BOOKS BY GAIL HAMILTON
A Candle to the Devil
Titania's Lodestone

A CANDLE
TO THE DEVIL

Gail Hamilton

A CANDLE
TO THE DEVIL

illustrated by Joanne Scribner

Atheneum 1975 New York

Library of Congress Cataloging in Publication Data
Hamilton, Gail.
A candle to the devil.
SUMMARY: The quiet Cornish seaport town seemed
peaceful enough until a painting was stolen, and
Daphne sensed hate and a kind of fear all around her.
I. Scribner, Joanne.   II. Title.
PZ7.H18156Can   [Fic]   75-9519
ISBN 0-689-30478-1

Published simultaneously in Canada by
McClelland & Stewart, Ltd.
Manufactured in the United States of America
Printed by Sentry, New York
Bound by Book Press, Inc., Brattleboro, Vermont
Book design by Mary Ahern and Kathy Westray
First edition

to *Barbara and Richard Gercken*

Note: Somerset Maugham once said that it was impossible for English writers to capture American speech accurately, or for Americans to capture English. Certainly the Cornish accent and rhythm and usage are beyond Americans. When an attempt is made to render Cornish speech here, it is only what Daphne thought she heard.

A CANDLE
TO THE DEVIL

1

Dear Bo:

I am writing this somewhere over the Atlantic Ocean. (Yes, in a plane, stupid.) I don't trust our revered parents to remember to fill you in, so I'll do it myself. Do you remember my ever speaking of Emily Rutherford? You probably don't, because I very seldom spoke of her, or even thought of her. But old Emily has achieved fame at last. Her family took her to Yugoslavia for a week, and after she got back to school, it turned out somebody on the flight home had come down with cholera. Panic set in, and not only Emily but our whole dorm was quarantined. But it just so happened that I wasn't there at the time, having gotten weekend leave to attend the wedding of your cousin and mine, Miss Augusta (Gussie) Perth. (You should have come, Bo. Six bridesmaids and champagne, and Aunt Mabel sobbed all through the service.) Anyway, Father said I could not go back to school for the rest of the spring term. "No child of mine," he said in his best justice-of-the-peace manner, "is going into that

3

plague-ridden miasma." Mother reverted to her May-fair accent, as you know she does in times of stress. She said, "Oh, bother! I cannot have the child underfoot three extra months. She breaks everything." They had a private conference, and the upshot of it is that I am en route to England to visit poor Aunt Daphne, who was totally unprepared but has agreed to "soldier on," as Mother puts it. Mother says since I am half English, it is high time I was exposed to English culture. The poor woman seems to think that at sixteen I can still be shrunk back into a shy English violet. (By the way, I've grown another two inches since you went back to college. I am now exactly five nine. Pray for something to happen to my pituitary gland.) So when you see me again, old brother, I may (?) be a charming cultivated English young lady who never knocks anything on the floor or crashes into people, instead of the (quote) wild Wyoming cowboy (unquote) Mother says I am now. I really haven't had time to sort out my reactions, it's all happened so fast, but I am afraid they tend to be dubious. Mostly for poor Aunt Daphne's sake. I guess it will be fun to swish around London, see shows, and even investigate whether you're right about opera being a good thing. Mother says the stores are marvelous—Harrod's, Liberty's, Fortnum and Mason, and all that. It may be a ball, but right now all I can think of is how much I miss my horse. I made Jake swear he'd take care of Arrow before anything else. I shall never learn to like tea. Please write. Get the address from Mother. Aunt Daphne's gallery is in Chelsea, but I think she lives in Kensington, wherever that is. I'll keep you informed.

Your loving Sis

2

Daphne put the letter to her brother into her purse as the stewardess announced the descent into Heathrow. She felt nervous and excited. She had never been to England, although her mother was English, and she had not seen her aunt for about five years. She remembered thinking Aunt Daphne looked like a gypsy, but her mother had said fiercely that of course her sister did not look like a gypsy in the least.

"Your aunt is an artist," she had said firmly. "Artists never quite look like other people."

Aunt Daphne was not a famous artist. She did unusual greeting cards and sometimes she illustrated children's books. She also owned a small art gallery in Chelsea, which had apparently done very well.

Daphne combed her hair and tried to rub off a spot left by a splash of Coke on her jacket. Her mother was right, she was impossible, always spilling and dropping and crashing. But it was because she had grown so fast—that and the fact that most of the time she was outdoors, where you didn't have to be so careful. She had grown up on her father's sheep ranch. It wasn't a huge ranch; he was a lawyer too, and he had to leave a lot of the running of the ranch to his foreman, Jake. Daphne and Bo had always helped out like regular ranch hands in vacation. And because they preferred the ranch, they had seldom gone anywhere on vacation. This was Daphne's first trip abroad.

She checked her seat belt, tightened it a little further, curled her long legs under her, and pressed her nose to the glass, to watch England coming up at her. But there was nothing to see. The plane was gliding through thick layers of fog. Her mother had always spoken of London fog as if it were some special, glamorous substance that gave you rosy cheeks, not like other fogs, but as far as Daphne could see, it looked like plain everyday fog.

After they landed, she bumped her head on the luggage rack as she got out into the crowded aisle. The passengers were kept waiting for what seemed like a long time. Daphne was tingling with nerves and excitement. What if she didn't recognize Aunt Daphne after all this time? What if Aunt Daphne didn't recognize her? She certainly didn't look like the skinny little kid her aunt had seen five years ago. She clutched her purse and her vanity case, trying not to step on the heels of the woman in front of her.

Someone behind her said in an English accent, "It's smashing to be back, isn't it."

And a man answered. "It always is. Though it's pouring buckets out there."

At last the line began to inch forward. The woman

7

behind her hit Daphne in the back with her purse. "Oh, so sorry."

Daphne said, "That's all right." They would probably say to each other later, "Darling, did you see that perfectly enormous American girl? Six feet if she was an inch." Daphne hunched her shoulders in the way that her mother hated, trying to look shorter. She hoped Aunt Daphne wouldn't think she was a barbarian. Her mother sometimes had a lot to say about American barbarism. Once Bo had said, "Mother, how can you stand it here? How is it you've never fled back to England?" After that it was quite a while before Mother criticized America again.

Bo had been in London once for a couple of days on his way to Paris. He had liked it, although there'd been a taxi strike and he had missed his plane. He was a second-year music major at UCLA. His ambition in life was to make violins, really good violins. Daphne thought it was an interesting idea— different anyway—but people in Wyoming thought it was really weird.

"What's the delay?" someone said to the stewardess.

With professional blandness she said, "Oh, a bit of a security check. All clear now."

Daphne thought of bombs and swallowed hard. She would not care to be blown up in a plane. Or anywhere else. That was one thing about Wyoming, nobody blew up your horse. She looked around

8

cautiously to see if anyone seemed furtive. Not a furtive face in sight.

Well, she was out now. She looked frantically for Aunt Daphne, but there was no Aunt Daphne. There were lots of soldiers, however, and men in plainclothes who stood around looking so much like plainclothesmen that even she noticed them. There didn't seem to be a lot of welcomers here, so perhaps Aunt Daphne was further along the route. Daphne was swept along with the other passengers toward the customs office. Bo had said that Customs hardly looked at him or his passport, but the young man with the stern jaw who examined Daphne's looked at her severely and then back again at the picture.

"Here on holiday, are you?" he asked, as if that were suspect.

"I'm here to visit my aunt," she said.

"How long do you plan to be here?" He turned the pages of the little green book back and forth as if looking for some secret code. Then before she could answer, he stamped it and thrust it at her.

"Where do I go now?" she asked him.

He was looking past her to the next customer. "Follow the green line if you've nothing to declare, red if you have." He was perfectly polite, but he seemed worried.

She found the green line and went through. Now there were people waiting but still no sign of Aunt Daphne. She began to feel panicky. There were soldiers wandering around everywhere. She had never seen so many.

As she stood there wondering what to do next, a young man came up to her. At first she tried to ignore his obviously interested inspection, but when that became impossible, she looked directly at him, intending to flatten him with one cold stare, as she had been taught to do with obnoxious strangers in her class in social mores at school. Instead she was fascinated.

He was small, and the first thing that came into her mind was that he looked like a faun. He was very dapper in a perfectly fitted dark gray suit with scarlet waistcoat, a white silk shirt, a large polka-dotted bow tie, a pearl-gray bowler hat, and a tightly folded umbrella, which he held like a magic wand. He gave her an enchanting smile.

"Do forgive me," he said, in a light tenor voice. "But *are* you Miss Daphne Pelletier from Wyoming, U.S.A.?" He gave "Pelletier" a very French pronunciation.

"Yes," she said. "Who are you?"

He gave the umbrella a twirl. "Ah!" he said, "that is a question to confound the seers. But for working, everyday, practical purposes, I am St. John Everett, friend and partner of that great lady, your aunt, Mrs. Daphne Allerton-Kent." He bowed from the waist. "And because I understand that this presents a puzzlement for Americans, I will explain straightaway that although my Christian name is spelled

Saint-John, or St. John, it is pronounced Sinjin. May I have your baggage checks?"

Bemused, she handed him the checks and then, when he looked puzzled, discovered she had given him stubs for the Strand movie theater in Casper. She rummaged through her purse until she found the proper checks.

"Splendid," he said. "What was playing at the Strand?"

She hurried along beside him. "I don't remember. I think . . . yes, it was Barbra Streisand."

With the point of the umbrella he cleared a path through the waiting crowd to the luggage ramp. "Oh, I adore Barbra Streisand. She must have had a very hard life, early on, to be so very funny, don't you think?"

"Pardon?" Daphne felt like Alice in Wonderland. She wanted to ask where Aunt Daphne was, but the opportunity didn't present itself.

"Haven't you noticed, it's those who have known real trouble and struggle who are the top comedians. What colors are your suitcases?"

"One is red leather. The other is a sort of plaid cloth deal. Here it comes . . ."

Expertly he hooked the umbrella through the handle and lifted the case off the moving belt. "And here is the red one, it is not?"

"Yes. Fine." She reached to pick it up, but he waved her off. He was so little, she was afraid the two bags would bowl him over, but although he

11

staggered slightly, he managed, his umbrella tucked under one arm.

"And you want to know, where is Aunt Daphne."

"I did sort of wonder . . ."

"She is in the parking lot, row AA, nil-five-three-zed." He walked rapidly toward the entrance. "Actually, nil-five-three-zed is part of her car license. I have memorized it over and over. I have no head for figures. RAF nil-five-three-zed, in row 2 of section AA. She would have come in, you know, but since her accident, walking is a bit of a problem."

"What accident?" Daphne put out her hand to open the door, but it slid open automatically.

"I forgot . . . she didn't tell you. Didn't want to alarm your mother. Her horse threw her last summer in Rotten Row, a nasty fall. Broke a hip. She's much better now, but it does give one pause, doesn't it? I mean if you're not safe in Rotten Row, where are you safe?"

"A horse can throw you anywhere," Daphne said.

"Yes, so I understand. Nasty beasts. Never could abide them."

Daphne was shocked. "I am devoted to horses. I have a beautiful gelding at home . . ." But she stopped. She couldn't talk about Arrow to someone who thought horses were nasty. It was odd, because otherwise he seemed so nice.

"I grew up in Birmingham," he said. "My dad owned a pub. We never got near a horse. Actually I'm sure they're much nicer than I think. It's probably inverted snobbery on my part." He put the cases down and rubbed his hands together. "Where is that blooming AA? Have I got us properly lost?" He looked around. "Ah, there it is. Carry on."

"Wouldn't you like me to carry one of the bags?" Daphne felt silly. She was much bigger than he was.

"No, no, no, wouldn't dream of it." He staggered on to the AA section. "There we are." He raised his voice. "Hi! Daphne, old girl!"

The door on the driver's side flew open, and Aunt Daphne climbed rather laboriously out of the blue Austin Mini. Daphne was relieved to see that although her aunt seemed stiff, she wasn't actually crippled. And Aunt Daphne did look like a gypsy. Her long, narrow face was brown and lined, and her piercing brown eyes were almost black. She gave Daphne a warm smile and held out her hands.

"My dear Daphne. So happy to see you. So glad to have you here."

"Thank you. It's nice to be here. Mother sends her love." Daphne felt self-conscious with this aunt whom she hardly knew, and who was probably, in spite of what she said, wondering what on earth to do with this hulking niece. But at that moment she forgot her feelings about her aunt because she looked up and saw a long row of army tanks driving slowly past the parking lot. She gasped. "What are they? Is there a war or something?"

"Just those beastly army people," St. John said, trying to get both of Daphne's bags into the tiny boot of the Mini, and failing. "Security, security."

A half-track lumbered down the airport road, grim-looking soldiers in camouflaged uniforms crowded into it. It was followed by an open truck with more soldiers. Daphne felt very much alarmed. Had she left peaceful Wyoming only to stumble into a war or a revolution or something?

Aunt Daphne dismissed the army with a wave of her hand. "Some visiting dignitary whom somebody might decide to take a potshot at, I suppose. It's so absurd, really. So obvious. If you wanted to assassinate someone or blow up Heathrow, you wouldn't drive up to the gate and go through a search and all that. What you'd do . . . St. John, darling, you get in back with the suitcase and Daphne can sit up here with me . . . What you'd do is something quite unexpected. In a helicopter perhaps, the way the IRA did. British military and police are splendid brave chaps, but they simply have no imagination. They will be done in some day by someone with imagination." She started the engine of the little car.

St. John leaned forward. "You mustn't think," he said to young Daphne, "that we are always in this deplorable state. Actually, you know, English bobbies don't even carry guns."

"Really?" Daphne said. "What do they do when they come across a dangerous criminal?"

St. John said, "By Jove, you know, I never really thought about it. I suppose they just chat him up a bit and take him round to headquarters."

14

"Actually, you know," Aunt Daphne said, "the criminal himself, the English criminal, I mean, would probably not have a gun either. For all we're such a nation of soldiers, the civilan element just doesn't think in terms of guns, wouldn't you say, St. John?"

"I really don't know." He sounded gloomy. "Violence makes me sick. I try not to think about it."

"St. John spent a year with the army in Belfast," Aunt Daphne said.

Daphne tried to imagine the fastidious little St. John in the violent atmosphere of Belfast, and failed.

"It was beastly," he said.

"He received a medal for bravery, but he forbids me to speak of it," Aunt Daphne said. "Tell me, dear Daphne, did you have a smooth flight?"

As the rain began to fall again, she turned on the windshield wipers.

"It was a very good flight," Daphne said. "But foggy as we came in, and they said it was raining buckets."

"Oh, it was," Aunt Daphne said, "but that comes and goes, you know." She pointed to the leaden sky. "This morning the sun shone for over two hours." She stopped at the gate, but the guard waved her on through. "You see? We could be very dangerous criminals. He doesn't check us because we look respectable, but the clever assassin doesn't look like an assassin. I think I really must write a letter to the *Times*."

St. John laughed. "You always say that but you never do it."

Daphne tried to see as much as she could as the little car raced toward the city. There were lots of huge black cars, all alike, that looked like hearses but turned out to be taxis. The little Mini, which Aunt Daphne drove with great skill, darted in and out like a lizard.

"If you will, drop me at the Victoria and Albert, darling," St. John said. "I'm to meet that chap who's after a Mondrian. He lives near the museum." And when Aunt Daphne whipped around the corner by the big museum and stopped, he said, "Thanks awfully. I'll see you shortly in Boscastle. Lovely to have met you, Miss Daphne, and I'm afraid you have to get out a sec, so I can extricate myself. . . ."

He and Aunt Daphne talked business for a moment, until a truck swung around the corner and blew an irritable horn. "Ta, love," he said. "Bye-bye, young Daphne. Enjoy the coast."

"Coast?" Daphne thought. "Boscastle?" What was he talking about?

As the car swung around the block, Aunt Daphne said, "I don't think I ever had time to tell your mother the latest events in my life. I've retired from the gallery. I'm still a silent partner, but St. John runs it now. And I sold the flat."

Daphne caught a quick look at Harrod's as the car passed it. "Oh," she said. "Where do you live now?"

16

"In a little village called Boscastle, on the Cornish coast. Rather wild and desolate, I'm afraid, but it has its charm."

Daphne's heart sank. There went Harrod's and Fortnum and Mason's, the Savoy for tea, the theater, the opera, the zoo. There went sophistication.

"I'm sure it will be very nice," she said bravely, trying to ease her cramped legs into a different position.

"Oh, it's heavenly. The ruins are superb. Of course the wind blows at gale force most of the time and it rains constantly, but there's no end of smashing graveyards and magnificent Bronze Age tombs. Fascinating country, really." She gave Daphne her quick, warm smile. "I like to say if it was good enough for Turner, it's good enough for me."

Daphne smiled wanly and sank a little lower on her spine. Turner who?

3

Boscastle, Cornwall, March 10.

Dear Bo:

You wouldn't believe it. You simply would not
believe it. You are imagining me dashing around
London, watching the Changing of the Guard,
wandering up Carnaby Street, mixing with the birds
and the Teddy boys. Well, dear brother, you are
totally, but totally wrong. I am on the North
Cornish coast in the above-mentioned village. We
arrived here two days ago. On the first day down,
the fog was so thick, I felt as if I were inside a
marshmallow. I think Aunt Daphne must have been
driving by radar. Then we stopped for the night at
Salisbury and suddenly the fog lifted and there at
the end of that funny medieval little street was the
cathedral. It was so beautiful, I thought I'd faint.
Aunt Daphne says Constable painted it a lot, and he
or somebody else called it a poem in stone. It is. You
must see it. I wandered all around inside and I was
really overcome. Statues of dead knights are

stretched out like real corpses on top of their tombs right there in the aisles of the church. And the cathedral itself . . . well, I can't explain it. I am enclosing a postcard but that doesn't do it justice. The next day we drove along the most narrow, winding roads you can imagine, sometimes in rain and fog, sometimes in sunlight. We went through towns that looked as if nobody had been there since William the Conqueror. Narrow streets, usually cobbled, with houses attached to each other that lean across the street, kind of. Inns (pubs) with names like the George and Dragon, or the White Hart. It's really another world. The countryside is terribly neat and tidy and cared-for and somehow domesticated if you know what I mean. It's terribly pretty, but I feel like a giant in a land of Lilliputians. I'm so darned big and clumsy, and everything here is so small-scaled, after Wyoming, and so proper. It's full of charm but it scares me. I'm afraid I'll break England into little pieces and never even notice I've done it.

Aunt Daphne drives along these terrible narrow roads like a cat, if a cat could drive. And finally after miles of waiting for the moment when we'd crash into something but of course never did, I nearly fainted with relief because she said, "We're coming into Boscastle now." It happened to be pouring rain at the moment.

She had been telling me about Boscastle. It seems Aunt Daphne's hobby is archaeology and history and all that. There were Neolithic people here about three thousand years ago. In case you're interested, dear brother, it's because she likes all this stuff that she moved down here, that and because she got this ancient cottage quite cheap. There are burial mounds left by Bronze Age people, and Aunt Daphne promises me faithfully that we shall dig through a few. Ugh! Her eyes shine as she tells me about the megalithic tomb at somebody's farm. (Aunt Daphne is really a darling, but she *is* odd.) Well, I'll skip over the Iron Age fellows and the Romans, and the Celts and the Saxons and the Normans, whom I have not sorted out at all. We come down to about a hundred years ago. This was a very busy port, before the harbor silted up, but best of all, it was a hotbed of pirates and rumrunners and practicing witches. Now if this were only a hundred years ago, things might get kind of interesting.

Anyway we started down this very steep, winding road that plunges right down to the harbor, past these old-looking stone cottages that look all alike, like a modern housing development, and we come to this hairpin turn and Aunt Daphne stops. She wants me to see the view of the harbor! Bo, get the picture. It is blowing so hard, the little Mini almost falls over. The rain slashes at the windshield (windscreen, we say here) so hard the wipers don't make a dent. And I'm supposed to look at the view. Well, I looked, but the only impression I got was of a very narrow neck of water that comes roaring in past high, wicked-looking stone cliffs, and a couple of boats that look like toys moored and bouncing in the water. "That's where the pirates and the rumrunners used to come in at night," Aunt Daphne said with a happy smile. She had her head right outside the window and she was getting soaked. "They had secret tunnels so they could bring in their loot. Oh, I wish I could paint that harbor and get it right!"

I said was it always this kind of weather. "Oh, no," she said, "sometimes the sun comes out. Charles Wesley said, 'I saw a strange sight, the sun shining in Cornwall.' So you see, it does shine." I thought Charles Wesley was one of her friends, but it turns out he said that in 1743. It was *that* Charles Wesley. She also quoted to me a reassuring little poem by an anonymous gentleman traveling in Cornwall in the seventh century. (Aunt Daphne knows everybody.) He said:

Storm and destruction shattering,
Strike fear upon the world.
The winds are out, and through high heaven
Their bacchanals are hurled.

So you see what kind of situation I'm in. Right now I am being called for tea (hate tea), so I'll write again another day, if I live.

Love,
Sis

4

The end of tea was marked by two events: the abrupt dying down of the wind and a knock at the door of Aunt Daphne's cottage.

"Would you see who it is, dear?" Aunt Daphne said, finishing off the last of the tea in the silver pot. "I do hope it's not the dustman complaining about the bin again."

It was only that morning that Daphne had discovered that the "dustman" to whom her aunt referred so plaintively was actually the trash collector. He was annoyed with Aunt Daphne because the cat across the street had learned how to dislodge the lid of the dustbin (trash can). Aunt Daphne had put a rock on it now, but she wasn't sure that wouldn't annoy him as well. "What if it falls off on his foot?" Aunt Daphne worried about things like that. She had not seemed reassured by Daphne's comment that if he was too stupid to get his foot out of the way, then tough luck.

Daphne opened the door. A rather small, stocky man stood there, in working clothes, a cap on the

22

back of his head which he didn't bother to take off. He had round red cheeks and black eyes that twinkled in what struck Daphne as a rather professional way, like a department store Santa Claus who knows it behooves him to twinkle.

"'Evening," he said, although it was only five o'clock. "Mrs. Allerton-Kent, if you don't mind." He said something else, but he had such a strong Cornish accent that Daphne could not understand him.

"Whom shall I say is calling?" she asked, and then wondered if you put it that way to tradesmen or whatever he was. It would never have occurred to her to think that at home, but she had noticed already that there were unmistakable differences in the way people of one station in life spoke to people of another station in life.

The little man gave her a grin—she wasn't sure whether it was friendly or mocking—and stepped past her into the tiny hall. "Mrs. Allerton-Kent," he called out. "Randall here."

Aunt Daphne came into the hall with her slight limp. "Oh, Mr. Randall of course. I forgot you were coming." To Daphne she said rather vaguely, "Mr. Randall is going to look to the eaves. We seem to have a bit of a leak, he thinks."

"I'll go right up then," Mr. Randall said, and he bounded up the very steep stairs like a much younger man.

Aunt Daphne looked at her niece rather help-

23

lessly. "Damp rot or something. The place is six hundred years old, you know."

Daphne had the feeling that Aunt Daphne didn't quite know how to deal with Mr. Randall either. "I'll clear away the tea things," Daphne said.

"Oh, don't bother, dear. I'd like to have you get outside while the weather is nice. You've hardly seen the town. Run along now and get a breath of fresh air."

Daphne suspected that her aunt was afraid she'd break the cups. But, relieved to be outside, she stood on the broad granite slab that made the front step, and looked around. It seemed very strange not to hear the wind howling and screaming and slashing away. The whole village appeared to be caught in a spell of stillness.

She looked down from the steep incline of the hill toward the harbor. The tide was out, and the boats were half heeled over in the mud. It was hard to believe that in a few hours the tide would come roaring into the narrow inlet with great speed and force, sending up showers of spray onto the lichen-covered rocky cliffs. She looked at the jetty that swung irregularly out into the channel, sheltering to some extent the boats on its inland side. She wondered if it had been there in the days of the pirates. She wished she could have seen a real pirate.

Above her the very narrow main street of the town climbed uphill, lined with old houses and shops. A small, rather battered van stood in front of the cottage, its front wheels pulled up almost to Aunt Daphne's garden wall. On the side of the van fading painted letters said RANDALL ENTERPRISES, J.R.C. RANDALL. She wondered what Mr. Randall's enterprises were, other than fixing leaks in people's attics.

She noticed that there was a youngish woman sitting in the van, fairly good-looking in an artificial way. Her hair had been bleached almost white and it stood out from her head like cotton candy. She was staring intently at Daphne. Daphne nodded but the woman didn't respond.

Daphne moved out of range of the woman's penetrating gaze, although she felt as if it followed her. Up at the curve of the street where Aunt Daphne's herbaceous border ended, a boy of about eight or nine was on his knees staring intently at the earth around the plants. He looked up as she approached. He had longish curly dark hair and a bright, impish face. He rocked back on his heels.

"Wot's yer nyme?" he said.

"My name? Daphne."

"Eh?"

"Daphne Pelletier."

"Wot?"

"My name is Daphne Pelletier."

"Cor!" He grinned.

"What's yours?"

"Nigel." He pointed toward the cottage. "B'long to the old lady, do you?"

Daphne bristled. "I am Mrs. Allerton-Kent's niece. She is not an old lady."

"Looks old t' me."

25

She wanted to squelch him, but there was something appealing about him even in his impertinence. She had a feeling he was teasing her, more than trying to be obnoxious. "What are you doing down there?"

"Slow wormin'."

"What?"

"Slow wormin'," he said impatiently.

"What's that?"

"Don't know what a slow worm is?" When she shook her head, he said "Blimey! You emmits don't know nothing."

"I suppose a slow worm is a worm that moves slowly."

"Nah. 'E's a lizard with no feet. I'll show you." He jumped over the border into a patch of soft dirt and started turning over the dirt carefully with his hands. He looked back at her. "'ee comin'?"

"No. I don't like lizards and worms. And Aunt Daphne will be mad if you mess up her garden."

"Ah, that!" He dismissed both her and Aunt Daphne with a wave of his hand. Then he pounced and in triumph held up a fat pinkish-gray wormlike creature.

Daphne shuddered and turned away. Just then Mr. Randall came out of the cottage. "Nigel!" he called. He said something else that Daphne didn't understand, but apparently Nigel did because he scampered to the van and quickly climbed into the back. The engine chugged, and the van drove off.

Daphne wondered if the woman was Mrs. Randall and Nigel their son. It looked like it. She walked on up the sharp ascent of the street in the eerie stillness. Wyoming had a lot of wind too, so she knew that experience of sudden calm after a high wind, but she had never encountered such strong winds at such force for so long a time, and with the added accompaniment of the beating sea and the fog and rain that slashed and drove at one as if they were alive. There was something very wild about the Cornish coast. She got the feeling, which she had never had anywhere else, that all those generations of men, right back to the Neolithic, were still somehow hanging around. When Aunt Daphne first showed her the cottage, she had said, "It's supposed to have a secret tunnel. And of course the place is haunted, like any self-respecting Cornish cottage that's over two hundred years old." It seemed to Daphne the whole town was haunted, although she didn't believe in ghosts. And even if she did, she wondered would they keep her busy for three months? What did one do in a Cornish town?

An elderly gentleman with a small military-looking moustache, wearing a raincoat and a checkered cap, passed her. He carried a cane in one hand and in the other the leash of his wirehaired fox terrier. He walked briskly and as he went by her, he touched his cap with the handle of his cane and said, "Evening," in a no-nonsense kind of way. She found him reassuring. He had probably fought bravely in the

27

something-regiment and had done his stint in India. She was sure he had no connections at all with smuggling, piracy, or the Bronze Age.

Up at the top of the hill she came upon an ancient-looking building, or collection of buildings, whose sign said it was the Napoleon Inn. She wandered into one of the narrow little alleys that separated parts of the inn. A sign there said that the inn dated from the sixteenth century, and that during the Napoleonic wars the owner had recruited men to fight off French invasion. Never a dull moment in dear old Boscastle, she thought. She pushed at the big oak door on her left and was startled when it swung open. The place had looked closed. She found herself looking into a low-ceilinged, beamed tap room with thick white-washed walls. Three men stood at the bar, and their heads swung around in unison as her push at the door let in the cold air. For a moment she thought they must be recruits for the army against Napoleon. None of them said a word.

Then the bartender said, "Either come in, love, or shut the door."

She shut the door hastily and went away. She could have sworn she heard ghostly laughter, but then she realized it was just the wind that had started to blow again. She hurried down the hill toward the cottage, her hair whipping around her face.

Aunt Daphne was sitting in the kitchen reading a letter while the peas boiled. "Come sit near the stove, dear," she said. "It's getting cold again, I'm

28

afraid. St. John sends you his best and says to tell you all that nonsense at Heathrow was just an IRA scare."

"IRA scare?"

"Yes, all that military display. Scotland Yard had had a warning that the IRA was going to shoot down a plane that some of the Ulstermen were coming in on, Ian Paisley, I believe and some other Northern Irish. Such nonsense."

Daphne didn't know whether she meant it was nonsense to think they would do it or nonsense of them to think of doing it. She said, "I don't understand Irish politics."

"Oh, my dear, if one did. Centuries of tumult." She put down the letter and stirred the peas and shut off the burner. "The Cornish are Celts, too, you know. I feel that is why they are hard to understand sometimes. They kept people out for such ages. Very isolated and clannish." She put some butter into the peas. "I wish I knew what Mr. Randall was doing in the cellar."

"Cellar? I thought he came to fix something in the attic."

"Yes. But I heard something . . . I assumed that cat across the street had got into the cellar again . . . so I went down to see. But there was Mr. Randall just coming up. He must have gone down the back stairs, which is really rather dangerous. They are in need of repair, and I wouldn't dream of using them."

"Did you ask what he was doing in the cellar?"

"I asked if he were looking for something. In that

blithe way of his, he said, 'Oh, no, madam. Simply checking the stairs. They want mending.'" She sighed. "I suppose I shall have to be firmer with him. He is really a bit cheeky. But he's always there, you know, when I need the dustbins taken out or the ashes sifted. Rather handy, really."

"I suppose he needs the work," Daphne said.

"I am sure he does. They live in that absurd abandoned hotel out on the cliff toward Crackington Haven. Just the four of them rattling around in that drafty old monster of a place with the wind howling about their ears. In the summer I believe they do tidy up a few rooms to rent to busloads of pensioners, but it can't really pay them."

"Four of them?"

"The man and his wife and their boy and the old mother. The mother has a reputation in the village for being a witch, but then, that is probably because she looks like one. In a few more years they'll say I'm a witch too, I have no doubt." She opened the oven door and speared the baking potatoes. "Not quite."

"Aunt Daphne, what's an emmit?"

"Emmit? It's rather an uncomplimentary Cornish slang word for tourist, or outlander. Did someone call you an emmit?"

"The Randall boy."

Aunt Daphne smiled. "Oh. Well, Nigel likes to tease. He's a good boy." Then she added thoughtfully, "At least I think he is."

5

Dear Bo:

It is very cold, and the wind is screaming. It screamed all night and I couldn't sleep. I had two hot water bottles and a duvet. Is anything looking like spring in Wyoming? It will be April pretty soon. But you're in California, aren't you—I forgot—and it's always spring in California, right? I wish somebody would write to me about my horse. I've asked and asked mother how he is but she never says. What if he died? Or ran away. Or was stolen. I wish I were home. I'd ride him faster than the wind, faster even than the Cornish wind, for a long way. Oh, I wish I were home.

Aunt Daphne is very busy. She got manuscripts for two books at once, that she has to do illustrations for, and she has been working away like mad. Even when she isn't actually working, you can tell she's thinking. She is very nice to me, never cross or anything, but when she's like this, I don't think she really knows I'm here. St. John is coming down this weekend so maybe things will be livelier for a couple of days. He's a funny little man, both funny-peculiar and funny-humorous. I like him. He sent me an enormous box of candy last week.

Mr. Randall is thumping around in the cellar to see if we have termites. How does he expect to tell? Does he expect a termite to rear up and say good morning? Actually it isn't termites. They don't have enough wood in Cornwall to give one termite a solid meal. What it is that Mr. Randall is looking for is "damp rising and slow rot." That's what he said. He spoke the words "damp rising" with ominous inflection, as if the whole house might fall about our ears. He seems to think Aunt Daphne was out of her mind to buy this house. He even offered to try and sell it for her. There was somebody else, some anonymous customer, who almost got it when it was up for sale, but Aunt D. outbid him. She wonders who it was because he was allegedly angry at losing it, but the estate agent wouldn't tell her. "Confidentiality of the client, madam," he said, "rules of the profession." The English set great store by rules. The bank wouldn't cash a check (cheque) for Aunt Daphne at first, even though they know her very well, because she left out her middle initial when she endorsed it. And she thought they were quite right. Maybe that's why England is such a civilized country, as everybody says it is—because of the rules. Think so? I don't think Cornwall is all that civilized though. No rules could tame this countryside.

Mr. Randall is making a great racket in the cellar.

He must be working on the back stairs, which no-body wants to use anyway. I can tell because the door from the back stairs to the cellar screeches when you open it. Aunt Daphne doesn't feel easy about Mr. Randall, but she can't think of any reason to get rid of him. Also I think she is a little afraid of making an enemy of him. I would be, too. She thinks he knows who tried to buy the house but he won't tell. Talk about clannish! I also think Mrs. Jones knows things. But about what? I don't know. It must be just the general air of mystery that they like to keep going.

Well, I shall go for a walk. There are lovely foot-paths all marked out for you but often it's just too wet to walk. So adios, old brother. Write when you have time.

Love,
Sis

6

Daphne put on her heavy sweater and her parka with the fleece-lined hood and pulled on the red rubber boots, the "Wellingtons," that Aunt Daphne had for her.

"Everybody needs Wellies in the country," Aunt Daphne had said. "I'm surprised your mother didn't remember."

Daphne had held out at first for her western boots, until she discovered how much squishy wet mud one had to slog through on a walk along the footpaths. Her boots would take a terrible beating in that gucky stuff. She and Aunt Daphne were keeping a list of words that baffled or amused each other in the other's speech. Before she left the house, Daphne thought of the word "gucky" and wrote it down on the list. She left a note for Aunt Daphne, who was working away upstairs in her study. "Gone for a little hike along the coast. Love, *Daphne*." She would probably be back before Aunt Daphne even came out of her study. Aunt D. had her own tea-making apparatus up there and sometimes she didn't come down all day. Daphne had already read most of the decent-looking books in the cottage and explored a lot of the territory around. If only there were someone she could do things with, whatever there was to do. But as Aunt Daphne said, the Cornish did seem to keep to themselves.

Mr. Randall was again thumping about down in the cellar, and as Daphne opened the door to the chilly wind she saw Mrs. Jones, the "daily", coming up the hill. Mrs. Jones was a nice, motherly person, who not only cleaned up but saw to it that the things Aunt Daphne might forget—like getting the groceries in before the shops closed on Wednesday afternoons —were taken care of.

When Daphne met her on the road, Mrs. Jones stopped, puffing a little after the climb. "Mornin', love," she said. "Shockin' weather, i'n it." She said the same thing every morning, except for the three times when she had been able to say, "Lovely weather, i'n it."

Usually Daphne didn't understand what Mrs. Jones was saying the first time around, but Mrs. Jones didn't understand her either, and they both laughed about it. One morning when Daphne had given Mrs. Jones some instructions from Aunt Daphne, Mrs. Jones had looked at her for a moment and then said, "I see you've not lost your American accent yet."

It wasn't just the accent, Daphne thought as she went on down the hill for her walk; it was the melody, so to speak. She had tried to explain it to Bo. "Where our voices go up, theirs go down, and vice versa." She had made a musical scale for him to match the English and the American versions of "Is there something that you want?"

She stopped at the greengrocer's and bought a pocketful of apples.

"Bit of a breeze this morning," he said.

Daphne, gasping from the wind, said, "Yes. Bit of a breeze."

At the corner she posted her letter to Bo in the pillar-box. Her mother still said "pillar-box" for mailbox, so that had not surprised her, but she had been surprised to find that it was literally a box built into a stone pillar that was part of a fence.

For a moment she hung over the stone bridge looking at the enormous water wheel and the closed-up shop that had once been an old mill. The wind beat at her back and the gray clouds piled up overhead. A dozen gulls swooped and glided and rode the wind. The gulls were around all the time, in all weather, whistling and calling and beating the air. She wasn't used to gulls in any numbers, although sometimes she had seen a herring gull or two in the plains. She loved them. They were beautiful. She watched them till her neck ached, and then crossed the Valency River and set off toward Penally Point, climbing up over steep rocks to the National Trust path. The wind took her breath away, and she had to stop often.

When she finally scrambled up to the top, she

stopped and pulled an apple from her pocket. The wind was dying down, which would make the walk easier, but rolls of mist were beginning to move in from the sea. Aunt Daphne had warned her not to get near the edge of the cliffs, even on a good day. She said they often looked safe when they were actually ready to fall away. The sea and the wind and the rain were constantly redesigning the shoreline.

Looking out at the misty harbor and chewing her very good apple, Daphne shivered and stepped back a little. It was a three-hundred-foot drop over rugged cliffs to the beach below, and a little farther on, the path rose up another hundred feet. Daphne thought about going back, but she really didn't want to hole up in the house again. In spite of the weather it felt good to be out in the cold, fresh, sea air. It woke her up. She decided to climb on up to the top of Pentargon.

A gull swooped close to see what she was eating. She threw the core onto the ground. In an instant five gulls and two gray-headed crows sailed down. They didn't fight over the core, but they hovered close to it, pretending no interest, but each one trying to move in a little closer. In a sudden fast grab, one of the gulls seized it and flew off. He dropped it, and the whole thing began all over again.

"I'm betting on you," Daphne said, to the gull who had gotten it first. She was right. He pulled off his trick a second time and flew away with the prize.

From the top of Pentargon the sea below her

looked black and wicked as it smashed against the rocks. She knew there must be a beach in the tiny cove, but Aunt Daphne had warned her to stay off the beaches because the tide came in with such unbelievable speed and force. Every summer, she said, people drowned because they didn't understand about the tides.

Daphne wished she could go down some time, though. There was a great monster of a cave down there, Aunt Daphne said, and a little waterfall that she couldn't see at all from where she stood. She was fond of caves, but she did realize that it would be terrifying, not to mention fatal, to be in one of these vast Cornish caves when the tide came pouring in. She shivered. Had pirates, she wondered ever been lost in those caves? It would be nice to see a pirate. Exciting. But not a drowned one.

She walked on a little further, the fog curling around her in wisps. At the point where she could either go up the coast to the eight-hundred-foot cliffs called The Strangles (a name which gave her the shivers) or cut back across the field to the village, she decided to be sensible. No point in falling off an eight-hundred-foot cliff in a blinding fog.

Again the absence of the wind, after the many hours of gale force, gave her an odd feeling of standing inside some kind of envelope of stillness. The fog curled and eddied, thickened and lightened, so that sometimes she could see quite well for a few minutes, and then she could hardly see beyond an

38

arm's length. The penetrating chill made her squirm down inside the hood of her parka.

She was startled, in a moment of lifting fog, to see gray shapes ahead of her. Then she realized they were sheep. She was glad to see them. She loved sheep. At home soon it would be lambing time. Here too, of course. She had had a pet lamb of her own almost every year.

She stood still, looking at the sheep. One old ewe pointed her black-nosed face toward Daphne and watched her, moving a few feet away every time Daphne took a step toward her.

"All right, old girl," Daphne said. "Don't worry."

The fog swirled around her again, and the sheep became only faint gray shapes, then invisible altogether. She hoped she could stay on the path. The ground was so muddy, her Wellingtons made squelching sounds as she stepped carefully along. She wished she were back at Aunt Daphne's. "Jolly good thing," as Aunt Daphne would say, that she had turned away from the cliff. The fog was really rolling in. It would be easy to lose one's direction.

Suddenly out of the fog, directly in front of her, a figure appeared, a weird skinny figure in a flapping coat, waving its arms and shrieking in a hoarse croak like a crow's.

Daphne yelped. The creature ran straight at her, yelling something. Daphne turned and started to run, but in a moment reason took hold and she stopped short. She had been running straight toward

40

the cliff. In anger she wheeled around to confront whatever it was.

The creature, and she saw now in a slight lift of the fog that it was an old woman, had turned away from her and was moving off toward the Strangles, shooing the sheep ahead of her. A thin shepherd dog circled the sheep. Daphne stood still, breathing hard. She felt like an idiot. She had let herself be scared, panicked, by an old woman who had mistaken her for a sheep—which seemed ridiculous. Perhaps the woman had thought she might frighten the sheep into running off the cliff. Daphne wondered if she should go after the woman and tell her she hadn't meant to scare the sheep, that she understood sheep herself. But something held her back. She had had a bad fright and she wasn't over it yet. Why would the woman want to drive her off the cliff? There were better ways of protecting the sheep surely.

Picking her way carefully along the path across the open field, she headed for home.

7

When she had come almost all the way across the field, a shout startled Daphne. It was close by, a high-pitched yell coming out of the fog. This time she resisted the temptation to run. She turned toward the sound and was thankful she had not made a fool of herself a second time. It was Nigel, standing on one foot in a pool of mud, balancing himself with a cricket bat. There was no boot on the upraised foot.

"What on earth are you doing?" she said. "Where is your Wellie?"

"Stook." He pointed to the black rubber boot standing in deep mud, its foot entirely out of sight. "It coom off." He gave her his impish grin. "Pull 'm out, there's a good myte."

Daphne couldn't help laughing. "All right, mate. Hold everything." She stepped gingerly, not wanting to lose her own boots in the same way. When she was close enough to reach Nigel's Wellington, she grabbed it and pulled. At first it refused to come, but she pulled harder, and it began to make gurgling sounds as it loosened.

42

Delighted at the scene, Nigel shouted, "Pull 'm 'ard, myte."

She gave a great jerk, and the boot came free in a wild splatter of mud and water. Daphne almost fell over backward. Her face and her parka were splashed with mud, but she held up the boot triumphantly. "Your boot, m' lord."

Nigel shouted with laughter. He hopped toward her and leaned against her while he pulled on the muddy boot. "Good job, myte." He patted the pocket of her parka. "Wot you got there?"

"Apples." She pulled one out and gave it to him.

"Thanks." He took a big bite. With the apple in his hand he gestured toward the cliffs. "Seen me nanny out there, did you?"

"Nanny?" She was puzzled.

"Ay, nanny, nanny." He mimicked her tone. "Don't know a nanny?"

"I thought a nanny was an English maid who took care of children."

He hooted. "Ain't no maid. Don't take care of me neither. Me nanny is me grandmother. Me dad's mum."

"Oh. No, I didn't see. . . ." She stopped. "Does she have sheep?"

"Sometimes." He slanted his eyes at her mysteriously.

"A person can't have sheep sometimes."

"Nanny can." He watched her face to see her reaction. "Me nanny's a witch."

"Oh, nonsense," she said. "There aren't any witches." But she felt a chill go up her back.

"No witches!" He looked genuinely astonished. "You emmits . . . you don't know nothing." He shot away from her, riding his cricket bat like a horse, and took off across the field. In a moment he was lost in the fog.

She called after him. "Why aren't you in school?"

His high, mocking voice came back. "Don't like it."

She walked home slowly, thinking about old women who thought they were witches. And old women who almost ran you off a cliff.

Aunt Daphne was in the kitchen having a cup of tea with Mrs. Jones.

"Ah!" cried Mrs. Jones. "Just in time for a cuppa, you are."

"And just in time to miss the rain," Aunt Daphne said, as rain suddenly splashed against the kitchen windows. Then she looked down with dismay at the streaks of wet mud and wisps of grass that Daphne's feet had left on Mrs. Jones's newly washed floor.

"Oh, I'm sorry. I've wrecked the floor." Daphne felt bad. Aunt Daphne was an extremely neat and clean woman, and she herself was far from such virtues. She tried awkwardly to wipe up some mud with a Kleenex, only smearing it in a wider pattern.

"Never mind," her aunt said quickly. "Why not get the Wellies off outside and come have a bit of tea."

44

"It'll wash up," Mrs. Jones said, with large good humor. "That's wot dirt's for, i'n it?"

Daphne went outside and took off her boots, angry with herself for not having done it in the first place. As her mother said, she never stopped to think.

When she came back into the kitchen, Mr. Randall had joined the tea break. He stood with his back to the sink, his feet crossed, surveying the ladies with his twinkling composure.

Daphne had washed most of the mud off her face and had hung up her parka in what Aunt Daphne called the tidying-up room off the kitchen, but she saw Mr. Randall's look of amusement at her dishevelment.

"Been out in a bit of breeze, eh?" he said.

She wanted to say, "I've been rescuing your child," but that might get Nigel into trouble. She wondered if Nigel played hookey or if he really just didn't go to school. Didn't people have to go to school?

As if she had read Daphne's mind, Aunt Daphne said, "I saw Nigel go by this morning. Is he out of school again, Mr. Randall?"

Mr. Randall touched his forehead with the palm of his hand in simulated distress. "Oh, that boy! Says it's too far to walk to school."

"Well, it *is* a bit of a hike, isn't it, from your . . . from where you live," Aunt Daphne said.

"Good for 'im. Strengthen his muscles. I walked twice that far when I was a lad."

Mrs. Jones gave a whoop of laughter. "Come off

it, Roger, come right off it! Never saw you in school, we did, from Guy Fawkes' day till the long hols."

Mr. Randall grinned. "Well, now, Alice, I didn't say where it was I walked to."

"And better not. And better not, indeed." She winked and wagged her head, and they both laughed as if they knew great secrets. "More tea, madam?" she said to Aunt Daphne. "You've worked that hard all morning, you do deserve it."

"Thank you, Mrs. Jones. You do make a nice cup."

In her mind Daphne agreed. She had come to England hating tea, but both Aunt Daphne and Mrs. Jones produced something very agreeable that even her mother couldn't approximate. But then, her mother hated to cook.

"How are you coming with the cellar, Mr. Randall?" Aunt Daphne asked. She took a sober tone with Mr. Randall, as if she felt there was danger in joining in his jokes.

"Getting to the root of it, madam," he said. "Doing nicely. But I hold small hopes."

With a hint of exasperation Aunt Daphne said, "That seems a bit contradictory, 'doing nicely' but 'having small hopes.'"

He explained in his soothing way, as if she were not quite bright. "Doing nicely getting at the cause of things. Having small hopes of being able to put it to rights."

"Oh, dear," she said. "Really?" She looked distressed.

"Six hundred years, the cottage. Not much good left in it. You'd do well, madam, to sell."

"Pay him no mind, madam!" cried Mrs. Jones. "What do men know? Always preachin' disaster, i'n it? The cottage is good for another six hundred, have no fear." She looked indignantly at Mr. Randall.

To her surprise, Daphne caught a flash of anger in Mr. Randall's eyes before he had time to disguise it with a superior smile.

"Women," he said, with a shrug. He finished his cup of tea and put it down with a clatter. "You make a fine bit of tea, Alice. Stay with your speciality." He put his cap squarely on his head and then shoved it back a little to give himself a jaunty look. "Off I go. Dustbins tomorrow, Mrs. Allerton-Kent."

"Yes," Aunt Daphne said rather absently. She watched him go out the back door. When he had gone, she said, "I wonder, you know, if he's right about the cottage. If I'm going to have endless expense and worry . . ."

Mrs. Jones gathered up the tea things. "I doubt he's right, madam. He's up to something."

Aunt Daphne gave her a quick look. "Up to something?"

Mrs. Jones's face closed. "Oh, some little scheme," she said vaguely. "A great schemer, Roger always was. Fancies to make himself indispensable to you, I shouldn't wonder."

"Perhaps so," Aunt Daphne said. She continued

47

for a moment to study Mrs. Jones's face but there was nothing more to be read there.

Daphne remembered again her aunt's saying "the Cornish hang together."

"I shall bring you something from the fishmonger, then," Mrs. Jones said, firmly changing the subject. "A nice bit of plaice?"

"Thank you," Aunt Daphne murmured. "Plaice would be lovely."

When Mrs. Jones had put on her thick coat and bustled off to the shop, Aunt Daphne said, "Did you have an interesting walk?"

"Yes, although it got quite foggy." Daphne told her where she had gone but she didn't mention the old woman. She was afraid she would sound absurd. She did tell her aunt about rescuing Nigel's Wellington.

Aunt Daphne shook her head. "The boy ought to be in school. He's a bright lad, but no one seems to care what becomes of him. It *is* an awfully long walk, and his father could take him in the van, but he won't be bothered. The country schools are so crowded, I'm afraid they don't take much notice if a child doesn't come regularly." She got up and gave her shoulders a little shake, as if shaking off a depressing train of thought. "One of my books is about witchcraft. Would you like to go to the Witches Museum with me this afternoon?"

Daphne was startled. "Witches Museum?"

"Yes, there's a very good one in town. It's not usually open at this time of the year, but the owner was kind enough to say I might look through it this afternoon. I've been there before, but not with an eye to using it. I need some sketches. Like to come? It's quite fun."

"I'd like to very much," Daphne said. She went upstairs to her room to change into dry clothes. The idea of a witches' museum seemed so odd, elevating witchcraft to some level of knowledge and culture that she had never thought of it as reaching. Well, it would be something to write to Bo about, and something more to do in Boscastle. She wondered if witch hunting were still a reasonable occupation.

8

Dear Bo:

If there's any little thing you'd like to know about
witches, just ask me. You wouldn't believe all I
know. I don't believe it myself. I thought witches
went out with Nathaniel Hawthorne or something,
but not in England. They are alive and well and very
busy. Yesterday Aunt Daphne took me to the Boscastle Witches Museum, because she has to do some
witchy-type illustrations for a kids' book. Well, it was
something. First let me tell you there's a notice outside the place that tells when the *present-day* witches'
coven meets, and where, just like it's the Ladies'
Aid or the Brownies.

So we knock (the place is closed until May 1)
and a very nice, perfectly normal English gentleman
lets us in, turns on the lights, and tells us to enjoy
ourselves. He disappeared, back to his office, I guess,
or maybe to some secret den. Aunt Daphne went
around taking notes and making sketches, so I was
left to myself. First there were cases of real stuff used
by real witches (usually identified on cards, just like

any ordinary museum). "Killing daggers," for instance, made of bone. A note says witches like to make their implements from living matter. Think about that one a while. And when something is labeled a "killing dagger," you don't for a minute see it as an instrument for opening the morning mail. Since these particular daggers belonged to particular witches, you look at them and speculate about who they carved up. They are wicked-looking blades, I might add. Then there are the pickled lizards, which they seem to dote on. I am not sure what they're for, but I suppose for spells. I used to laugh at the witch scene in "Macbeth,"—you know, all that about fillet of fenny snake, eye of newt, toe of frog, lizard's leg, and so on. I thought it was a joke, but Bo, it is no joke! I saw with my own eyes the pickled liver of a sheep, and the lizards, and all kinds of horrid things. Bottles of feathers are very big, and broomsticks made of twigs—they really do have broomsticks, just like in *The Wizard of Oz* and all the other storybook witches.

There are lots of wax heads made to put a spell on people. Beeswax is the best thing to make a figure or a head out of. If you want to shut somebody up, you make a beeswax head and put a needle through the lips. Great fun! A dandy place to cast a spell is under a whitethorn tree at a crossroads, of course at night. The roots of the whitethorn are supposed to come from the stakes driven into the graves of suicides, who were usually buried at crossroads and were not approved of by society or the church. Somebody named Bucca-dhu, who had a bunch of hounds with no heads, used to check up on these graves to see if any spirits were wandering around loose. But I digress. Except, while speaking of night wanderers, I want to alert you to the problem of witch-hares. Some sneaky witches disguise themselves as hares. If you come across a witch-hare, shoot him with a silver bullet. And to be sure the spell is broken, go home and start your trip all over again.

The way a person becomes a witch is interesting. Actually there are a number of ways. One of them, in Cornwall, is to go some place like Bodmin Moor where they have these rocking stones, also known as logan stones or logging stones or menhirs. These are huge granite rocks put one on top of the other, during the Bronze Age, something to do with burial rites, Aunt Daphne says. Anyway I guess they are fantastic, because they are so carefully balanced that you can touch the top one (if you can figure out how to reach it) and it will rock but it won't fall off. All those centuries! Anyway if you want to be a witch, all you have to do is touch the rocking stone nine times. Presto! you're a witch!

At least that's one way. But the really accepted method is when you're considered to be ready for it, you're left alone in an isolated room like in a cave or some place eerie like that. In this museum there's a big life-size room of this type, behind glass, with a life-size (and very realistic) girl getting the treatment. It scared me right out of my wits because I came upon it unexpectedly, and it was lit up with a red light. The character that wants to be a witch (and they are often quite young and pretty, apparently, from pictures of famous witches) is spread-eagled on an altar that looks like a real altar with the candles and the decanter of wine and all. She has to stay there until she is (or is not) visited by . . . I guess . . . the devil. The program notes or whatever you call them that are in the exhibit say that the young woman quite often goes mad. She is left there by another witch, and I guess there's no way she can get out until her time is up. She often shrieks and moans and who knows what. The red light is dim and scary.

Would-be witches have other little tests to pass, just like Boy Scouts. One of them is: a net, called a witch's cradle, is spread out over a fire and I guess she has to cook in that a while; I wasn't too clear about that one. But here's one that's very clear: a net is stretched between cliffs (this one is very popular in Boscastle). The witch, stripped naked except for a broomstick, which she uses for balancing, has to leap from one cliff to the other. If she's lucky, she makes it. If she's only half lucky, like Evel Knievel, she falls into the net. If she's really lucked out, she misses both cliff and net, and there's one more body cluttering up the Cornish seas.

There are lots of horned masks, and candelabras made of horn. There are boy witches too, dear brother, so don't feel discriminated against. As you probably know, in your great wisdom, they're called warlocks. They wear white robes that look like monks' robes. At least, the models in the museum did.

If you want to know the truth, the whole business is quite nasty and unpleasant. As I said, I used to think it was a joke, but now I know it's quite real and current, it gives me the shivers. It's quite porno, with lots of phallic symbols that even I noticed. And of course very antireligious. A witch has to learn to say the Lord's prayer three times backward, and take of wine, like in holy communion, but she keeps the bread and gives it to a toad. This seems to me quite nasty, but also kind of unrealistic because I have never seen a toad here. Maybe I just don't know their haunts.

I've got to close now because it's time for tea. One parting word of advice: if you want to avoid being ill-wished by a witch, keep a newly baptized baby in the house, or nail a horseshoe to the door, or throw some bread over your shoulder and spill a little beer. And if you get the whooping cough, kill a mouse, roast it to a cinder, crush it into powder, add milk and drink it.

Your devoted *Sis*

9

Daphne sat huddled up to the electric fire in the little living room, rereading a letter from her father in which he gave her a report on the "health and happiness" of all the animals, from her horse Arrow to the new litter of kittens in the barn. All were well, and her rabbit, Hopping John, had become "sentimentally attached" to one of the ewes and followed her everywhere. Daphne smiled and put the letter in her pocket. She wished she could see the rabbit and the ewe. The sheep, her father said, was very patient about the whole thing.

It was only 5:30 but it was dark in the house. Rain beat against the windows, and the wind shrieked. She hated to turn on the lights so early. The English were careful about "ell-ectricity." She went to the window and looked out at the rain-soaked street. One adventurous gull tipped and sank and struggled up again, trying to defeat the wind.

From the kitchen came the low voices of Aunt Daphne and Mrs. Jones. Because St. John was coming, Mrs. Jones had come back to help with dinner and the cleaning up. There was a roasting duck in the oven, and Daphne wrinkled her nose at the heavenly smell.

Out on the street Mr. Randall suddenly appeared, his yellow fisherman's oilskin coat flapping around him. Mrs. Jones said Mr. Randall had a boat and sometimes went out fishing in the late spring and summer when the seas were calmer. Daphne had heard Mrs. Jones asking him if she hadn't seen him out last week one evening, "in seas that would sink a pirate." But Mr. Randall had insisted it was not he she had seen. Daphne bet it had been, and wondered what he was up to. There was something decidedly odd about Mr. Randall. About his whole family for that matter.

Daphne watched him as he struggled with the dustbins, one by one, fighting the wind, rolling them on their rims to the house. He disappeared in the garden and in a few minutes she heard the thump and crash as he maneuvered them down into the cellar. You never knew when Mr. Randall would show up. Aunt Daphne liked to have the dustbins brought in in the morning, after the dustman had come, because she thought they looked ugly sitting out in front of the cottage. Mr. Randall always assured her that he'd come in the morning, but he came when he felt like it.

A car turned into the narrow street and came slowly up the hill. It was a blue MGB. The driver came to a stop just down the street and rolled down his window to peer at the houses.

Daphne shouted. "Aunt Daphne, he's here! St.

John is here!" She ran into the hall, grabbed her macintosh, and went outside to signal him up the street. According to Aunt Daphne, he had been here only once before, when she had first found the cottage and hadn't yet bought it.

Daphne waved her arms and he returned the wave, sticking his head out into the rain and shouting, "hello!" He parked and got out and gave her a hug, as if he had known her for years. She felt very glad to see him.

"Beastly weather!" He had to shout to make himself heard above the wind. He swung a small suitcase out of the boot of the car.

Mr. Randall materialized beside him. "Help you with the bag, sir?"

St. John raised his eyebrows but he only said, "Splendid. Thank you very much." He handed the bag to Mr. Randall and reached into the car for a package carefully wrapped in a waterproofed cloth. The package was about three by four feet, and St. John handled it with great care. When Mr. Randall reached for it, St. John shook his head. "I'll manage this one, thanks very much."

Mr. Randall gave the package a sharp look but he nodded and went into the house with the suitcase. St. John followed Daphne. She caught at the door as it banged in the wind. Aunt Daphne, smiling, stood in the hall to greet St. John as he came in and the door crashed shut behind him.

"My dear!" Aunt Daphne said, "I'm so glad you're here."

"Like English peppermints," St. John said, "Cornish weather is curiously strong." He put his package carefully on the floor, leaning it against the wall, and kissed Aunt Daphne on the cheek. "Lovely to see you. You're looking marvelous." He glanced up at Mr. Randall, who stood half way down the stairs. St. John rummaged in the pocket of his coat and picked out a fifty pence piece. He held it up. "Thank you."

But Mr. Randall shook his head emphatically. "Oh, no, sir. Not at all. Are you sure I can't help you with the package?"

St. John said, "No, thank you." He patted the top of the package and said to Aunt Daphne, "Wait till you lay your eyes on this, darling. I come bearing treasure."

Aunt Daphne looked excited. "From the weekend at Lord Sortwell's? It *was* a good weekend?"

"Superb. Simply superb. A find, I might say. Our colleagues around town are green, my dear, purely green with envy."

"Not the Mondrian?"

"No. They won't part with it. But this is a little something that turned up in the attic. Nobody has known, for God knows how many years. . . ." He stopped and glanced up at Mr. Randall, who still stood on the stairs.

"Oh, Mr. Randall," Aunt Daphne said, remembering him, "I think that's all. Thank you for coming out in this weather."

Mr. Randall nodded and came down the steep steps. "I shall come by tomorrow then, to fix that gate."

"I think it can wait till warmer weather . . ." Aunt Daphne began, but Mr. Randall was already letting himself out the front door.

St. John looked after him briefly. "Bit of a cheeky piece of goods, isn't he?"

"Very. But he does do things I can't get anyone else to do."

St. John peeled off his heavy coat and hung it on the hall clothes rack.

"Come sit by the fire and warm up," Aunt Daphne said, "before you do another thing. Even before you reveal your surprise. I'll fix you a gin and tonic. Daphne, dear, look after him, will you?"

Daphne pulled up the antique rocking chair close to the electric fire. "This is the haunted rocking chair, you know. It came with the house."

"Marvelous. How haunted?"

"Oh, people keep seeing it rocking as if someone has just gotten out of it, when no one is there. In my opinion it's just a draft."

He laughed. "You American skeptics." He sat down in the chair and rocked it a little. "Haunted or not, it's blessed comfortable."

"Yes, I think it's the most comfortable chair in the cottage. There's a story about a secret tunnel, too, but I haven't seen any signs of one."

He tipped back and looked at her. "So. How do you like Cornwall?"

She hesitated. "It's a little hard to say. It's very interesting, but it's hard to see much through all the wind and rain and fog."

He listened to the wind for a moment. "Yes. I can see that. Cornwall is a wild country. It never seems like England, quite, you know? More like some magic land left behind by the little people . . . or perhaps not "left behind". . . perhaps they're still here."

Daphne smiled. "I don't really think so." She settled comfortably on the squashy cushion on the floor. "How is London?"

"Marvelous. I never get over London." He looked around the room. "She's done wonders. This was really quite a dreary cottage when she bought it. I thought she was quite mad."

"It still seems mad to me," Daphne said. "When a person could live in London . . . Not that I know London . . ."

"Everybody knows London, whether he's seen it or not. It's part of a civilized person's heritage. Like Rome and Athens." He stretched his feet toward the electric logs. "It's a pity she couldn't have a real fireplace. I loathe those phony plastic logs."

"Why couldn't she?"

"Mainly because wood is so hard to come by in Cornwall. If you've noticed, everything is made of stone. That dreadful slate."

Daphne rather liked the Cornish slate but she refrained from saying so. She was sure St. John's taste was far superior to hers. In fact, she wasn't sure she had any.

Aunt Daphne came in bringing the gin and tonic for St. John and sherry for herself. "Daphne dear, orange smash? ginger beer?"

Daphne jumped up. "I'd love some ginger beer. I'll get it." She had been surprised to find that ginger beer was a soft drink, like ginger ale only more gingery. She liked it.

Mrs. Jones, looking hot and a little rumpled, was poking at the duck. She glanced up at Daphne. "Oh, I do hope it'll do for him. Him from London and all."

"He'll love it, Mrs. Jones. Nobody could help loving it. It's the best-smelling duck I ever smelled." Daphne got a bottle of ginger beer from the tiny refrigerator.

"I do hope so." Mrs. Jones closed the oven door and hovered over the hot stove a moment anxiously. "Salad," she said. "Fix the salad next."

"Can I help?" Daphne asked.

"No, dear, bless your heart, I'll manage."

"The dining room looks beautiful."

"Ah, that's your aunt's touch. A true artist, she is." Mrs. Jones got a head of lettuce from the refrigerator and began to shred it into a bowl.

There was a knock at the kitchen door. Mrs. Jones looked up, her hands full of lettuce. Daphne, who was nearest to the door, said, "I'll get it." She put down the glass that she was pouring the ginger beer into, and opened the door. The inrushing wind banged a cupboard door shut. Daphne squinted her eyes, trying to see who was standing there in the dark.

" 'Evening," the man said. He was a youngish man in a wet macintosh and a plaid cap. "It's a chap named Randall I'm lookin' for. I was told he might be here." His manner was pleasant enough, and his accent was Irish.

"He went home about half an hour ago. . . ." Daphne began. She stopped because Mrs. Jones had moved in. Mrs. Jones was far too polite to push, but Daphne had the distinct impression that she had been gently elbowed aside.

"Randall's only the handyman here," Mrs. Jones was saying in a rather stern voice. "It's not here you'll find him."

Daphne saw the man glance quickly around the kitchen, taking it all in.

"Ah, they were mistaken then," he said, but he still stood there, smiling at Mrs. Jones with what seemed to Daphne a peculiar smile.

"Mistaken they were." Mrs. Jones shut the door firmly. She shot the bolt that locked the door.

"I wonder who that was?" Daphne said.

Mrs. Jones gave her a quick look and went back to the salad. She seemed distracted. "Somebody lookin' for Randall," she said.

"Mr. Randall has a lot of irons in the fire, doesn't he." Daphne knew she ought to leave Mrs. Jones alone, but she was curious. The man apparently had not been someone Mrs. Jones knew, and even in the short time she had been in Cornwall, Daphne had learned that strangers were automatically suspect, unless they were obviously tourists. Still that was no reason for Mrs. Jones to be so obviously upset.

Mrs. Jones shrugged at her question. "A man needs a lot of irons to survive in this country." She turned away from Daphne, who took the hint and went back to the living room with her ginger beer, wondering still about Mr. Randall's irons.

St. John was carefully unwrapping the package he had brought, and Aunt Daphne stood by the fire watching eagerly. Daphne waited in the doorway as St. John slipped off the last of the wrappings. Dramatically he stepped aside, revealing a watercolor of a rugged coastal scene, framed in an ornate gilt frame.

Aunt Daphne gasped. "No!" she said. "It can't be."

"Yes, it is. I had it looked at in London to make sure." St. John beamed at her. "Hard to believe, isn't it? And yet when you remember that the man left more than 19,000 watercolors, drawings, and oils to the Tate and the National, it's not so amazing that there might be one or two tucked away that no one knew about."

Aunt Daphne went close to the painting and ex-

63

amined it carefully. "Didn't the Sortwells know?"

"Apparently not for the last several generations. Somehow it got stashed away—you know how that happens in those big homes. Somebody decides to redecorate and things go into storage. Young John happened to come across it and thought he had something."

"And he let you get it?"

St. John looked contrite. "I did take a bit of an advantage. But he wanted a quick sale. . . ." He grinned. "And he got it. I must tell you, love, I had a bit of a time scrounging up the necessary funds."

"I should think so. Of course it's not as if it were a Giotto or something. . . ." Aunt Daphne bent closer. "He isn't what he was forty years ago. But still. . . ."

Daphne was unable to control her curiosity any longer. "What is it?"

"Oh, sorry," St. John said. "It's a Turner. An unaccounted-for Turner. Most of them are in the national galleries. He did quite a bit of work in this area, actually in Boscastle itself. I don't think this is Boscastle, though, do you?" He asked the question of Aunt Daphne.

"No, but it is certainly Cornwall." She peered at it closely. "It might be Clovelly . . . I'm really not sure. I don't know that coast well enough. But, oh, St. John, what a find!"

He grinned happily. "I know you'd be excited. It should sell instantly and make us a lovely profit."

Aunt Daphne sat down and looked at it lovingly. "I wish I could afford it myself. It's very nice, isn't it."

"Yes, quite," St. John said. "Though as you know, I am not a great Turner man." He turned to Daphne. "Do you like it?"

"Yes," Daphne said. "It looks like Cornwall."

"Indeed it does."

They all started as Mrs. Jones's timid voice came to them from the doorway. "Dinner is ready, madam."

"Dinner! I'd almost forgotten." Aunt Daphne got up. "Where shall we put it?" She tried it on a small mahogany table, leaning it carefully against the wall. "There's too much in this room for it, of course." She turned around. "How do you like it, Mrs. Jones?"

"It's a very pretty picture, madam," Mrs. Jones said uncertainly.

"It's by a great early nineteenth-century English painter named Turner," Aunt Daphne said. "He did some paintings of the Boscastle Harbor. You've probably seen them reproduced in the souvenir shops."

"I never go in the souvenir shops, madam," Mrs. Jones said apologetically.

"Sensible woman," St. John said.

Daphne looked closely at Mrs. Jones to see if she resented what seemed to Daphne to be a patronizing tone from Aunt Daphne, but Mrs. Jones seemed quite serene. It must be the English way. Daphne could imagine Jake's reaction if her mother under-took to explain to him who Turner was. He wouldn't know any more about Turner than Mrs. Jones did, probably, but he would not take kindly to being instructed in that superior way. Aunt Daphne was a darling, but she was English all right. But I'm half English myself, Daphne thought, so it must be a matter of the society you grew up in, rather than what your blood lines were. She'd have to ask Bo what he thought about that. It was a new idea to her that people whom one thought of as being more or less like oneself, in this case actually related, would have quite different attitudes and behavior.

St. John was suitably impressed by Mrs. Jones's roast duck and told her so. She beamed and perspired and fled to the safety of the kitchen. "Humble" was the word, Daphne thought; and she laughed in her mind at the idea of Jake as humble. And yet Mr. Randall and even young Nigel were certainly not humble either. Maybe it was just differences in people. She stopped thinking about it and listened to St. John's entertaining account of a boring play he had been to with a client.

After dinner Aunt Daphne and St. John went "pub-hopping," as St. John called it, because Aunt Daphne wanted to show him both the Napoleon Inn and the Wellington, because of their age. Daphne couldn't go because of the law about minors.

She went up to her room after a while but she got bored and began to wonder if there really was a tunnel somewhere. Her few brief expeditions in search of one had proved fruitless. She decided to try the back stairway. Aunt Daphne had said it was dangerous, but Mr. Randall had allegedly been fixing it. Anyway she'd be careful. And if she got stuck or anything, she could holler for Mrs. Jones, who was still clattering around in the kitchen.

Taking her "torch," she slid the old bolt on the door and flashed her light down the stairs. They were narrow and a couple of them were broken, but they didn't look too bad. If there really was a tunnel—not that she believed there was—maybe it would connect with these stairs somehow. She started down cautiously. She had never really searched the cellar. Maybe it would be full of interesting treasures.

At the bottom she had to push hard on the creaky door, but it finally gave with a rusty screech. She thought for sure Mrs. Jones would hear her, and maybe be frightened, but Mrs. Jones was washing dishes and singing a lusty version of the Cornish anthem:

> *Trelawney he's in keep and hold,*
> *Trelawney he may die;*
> *But here's twenty thousand Cornish bold*
> *Will know the reason why.*

Daphne had heard her sing it lots of times although she had no idea what it was about.

The cellar was dark and damp, with a hard-packed

dirt floor. Parts of a big cupboard that Mr. Randall was making for storing preserves leaned against one wall. There was a lot of stuff in the cellar, though Aunt Daphne had obviously tidied up. Empty wine and whiskey bottles were stored in boxes, apparently destined for the dustman. Some old earthenware jugs stood on shelves. Part of a broken tombstone dated 1723 leaned against the wall, one of Aunt Daphne's treasures. And there were tools, a broken lawnmower, a wheelbarrow, the usual litter to be found in an old cellar.

Daphne flashed the light slowly along the walls. There was nothing she could see that looked like the entrance to a tunnel. If there ever had been one, it had probably long ago been filled in. It would be handy, though, she thought, if you were a nineteenth-century wine merchant and you wanted to smuggle in a lot of stuff from the sea. A boat could come into the harbor, or one of the coves, if the skipper was good enough to make it without crashing, and you could take the stuff from the sea to this cellar without anybody ever seeing it. What a fun age to live in.

She flashed her light up at the little window where the cat probably came and went. A small pane of glass was missing. Well, Aunt Daphne wouldn't have mice to worry about.

Suddenly she felt a cold chill go up her back. Someone was in the cellar behind her. She was certain of it although she heard no sound at all. She made herself stand still.

"Who is there?" she said.

"Why, Miss Daphne, is that you?" It was Mr. Randall. He sounded upset, not his usual cool self. "What in the world are you doing down here?"

She turned to face him, angry at having been frightened. "What are *you* doing here?"

"I needed my saw." He picked up a small saw from the half-built cupboard. "Doing a bit of repair work at home. I'm sorry I startled you. But you took me aback too, you know."

Daphne glanced at the stairs leading to the kitchen. "How did you get down here? You didn't come down the stairs."

For just a second he hesitated. Then he said smoothly, "I come down the back stairs. Thought I'd left my saw on the stairs this afternoon when I was working on 'em. Then I remembered . . . here it was. Well, I'll be going now. Good evening to you." He went up the kitchen stairs.

The sudden light as he opened the kitchen door made a yellow shaft into the cellar. Daphne heard Mrs. Jones give a little shriek of surprise and then their voices chattered together. The back door opened and closed.

"I'm down here, Mrs. Jones," Daphne called. "Don't close the door." She started up the kitchen steps. She looked back once at the door of the back stairs. It was closed, as she had left it. If Mr. Randall had come down the back stairs, why hadn't the door shrieked when he opened it?

10

Daphne woke to a strange sensation. Warm sunlight filled her room. She got up quickly, anxious to enjoy it before it went away.

Aunt Daphne and St. John were already at breakfast when she came downstairs. St. John jumped up to pull out her chair.

"Good morning! Sunshine is here!"

"I know. I couldn't believe it."

"We must have a picnic, quickly, while it lasts," Aunt Daphne said. She looked pleased and happy. "Mrs. Jones is fixing us a lovely lunch."

"That sounds wonderful." Daphne felt happy, too. The sunshine was like some warm, delightful stimulant. It made the whole world look different.

"Where shall we go?" St. John asked.

"First I want to take you up the coast. Perhaps we could picnic at the Strangles." She laughed as St. John made a joke of choking. "It's really beautiful on a good day. Then you should see the Thomas Hardy church, and if the weather holds, a quick trip to Bodmin moor perhaps. You've never seen the Stripple Stones."

70

"Hold on," St. John said, passing the broiled kippers to Daphne, who politely refused. "Why did Hardy have a church? He didn't get into the ministry, did he?"

"But my dear, he started out as an architect. He restored a lovely little church, St. Juliot's, not far from here. He fell in love with the vicar's daughter, in fact, and married her. There was a church there in the thirteenth century but actually except for a few things, some carved masonry and what was probably the original font, most of it is a nineteenth-century restoration. It's still lovely, though, and if you're interested in Hardy. . . ."

"I am," Daphne said. "I read *The Mayor of Casterbridge* for English last year and I loved it." She felt pleased at being able to join the conversation on this intellectual level. She did want St. John to think of her as a grownup and sophisticated.

"I like him, too," St. John said. "What are the Stripple Stones?"

"It's a Stone Age henge . . ."

"As in Stonehenge?"

"Yes, the same sort of thing. A stone circle with a ditch outside it . . . No more eggs, thank you, Mrs. Jones . . . Neolithic, they think."

"In dates, what would that be?" St. John said. "I am horribly ignorant about these things."

"Somewhere in the 3000 B.C. period."

"Wow!" Daphne said. "I thought the Plymouth Rock was old."

They both laughed. "In Cornwall," Aunt Daphne

said, "you really have to stretch your mind to en-
visage the people and the life that went with the
remains we still see all around us."

After breakfast they packed the picnic hamper into
the tiny boot of Aunt Daphne's Mini and set off.
Daphne wished they could have gone in the MGB,
but it had only two bucket seats. She curled her long
legs under her in the back seat and listened to Aunt
Daphne and St. John talk about all sorts of exciting-
sounding people and places in London. She wondered how Aunt Daphne could stand to be buried
down here in the country.

Aunt Daphne drove at her usual rush of speed,
and Daphne held her breath as the little car swooped
up and down hills and around long curves on the
road that was sometimes wide enough for just one
car. Coming down from London she had asked her
aunt what happened if she suddenly met another car.
"One backs up," Aunt Daphne had said.

The high hedgerows that cut off much of the view
of the fields were sprinkled with yellow gorse, which
Daphne had discovered was very prickly. Nature in
England seemed to Daphne quite different from the
Rocky Mountain area; in England it was pleasant
and safe-looking, as long as you stayed away from the
shoreline. In Wyoming the beauty always held a
threat of danger. Daphne liked Wyoming best,
dangerous or not.

As they drove along, Aunt Daphne stopped
abruptly here and there to point out an old Norman

church tucked away in a lane, or an old farm that had a fourteenth century church font in the field, hollowed out to make a pig trough. They were out of sight of the sea most of the way, but finally Aunt Daphne turned onto a narrow coast road that led up to the place called The Strangles.

They had to park and walk in, Aunt Daphne leaning on her hawthorn walking stick and holding to St. John's arm. The Strangles this morning reared up high above a shining sea, the violently twisted rock formations giving it the look of some enchanted world. Far below them was the beach with the two big sea arches called North and South Door. Daphne looked down from a safe distance and shivered. It was beautiful but frightening. Why had she just thought that English landscape was safe-looking? That was only when you were on the safe side of the hedgerows. Always, over here, there was the sea, ready to smash. But today it looked serene and smooth, as if no wind had ever churned it up into shattering, boat-breaking waves.

While St. John went over to peer into the deep chasms made by strange, precipitous rock cliffs some yards away from the coastline, Aunt Daphne pointed out to Daphne the old hotel where the Randalls lived, almost hidden by a dip in the shoreline. Daphne walked toward the meadow to get a better look. It was a rambling, big structure, incongruously roofed with thatch as if someone had tried to make it look like an enormous English cottage. As she got closer,

Daphne saw that it was four stories high, sprawling widely, with illogical turrets breaking the outline in a random pattern. It was not quite as close to the edge of the cliff as it had looked, so it was probably not in danger of collapsing into the sea, as it had seemed at first. She was glad of that; she wouldn't want to have to worry about Nigel getting washed away.

She shaded her eyes with her hand and studied the place. A row of trashcans were lined up at the back, and there was a rusting auto body and a bicycle. As she watched, Nigel's mother burst out of the back door and ran around the far side of the building. Then the grandmother appeared in the doorway, yelling something. Daphne decided she had better go back.

When she had taken a few steps, she turned aside to speak to a pair of sheep who were industriously cropping the grass. But as something rose up out of the grass at her feet, she gave a small shriek and nearly fell as she jumped aside.

It was Nigel. He had a long spyglass in his hand. "Wot 'ee yellin' about?" he said, rather crossly.

"You scared me. What are you doing with that thing?"

"Spyin'."

She looked in the direction he was facing and saw Aunt Daphne and St. John bending over a rock formation. "Are you spying on my aunt?"

He nodded and put the glass to his eye again.

"That's not very nice, spying on people."

"Wot's a spyglass for?" he said.

"Well, it's for somebody out at sea, looking for other boats and things."

"Not lookin' for nobody out to sea. Not right now." He gave her a shrewd glance. "You was spyin' on me house."

Daphne flushed. "I was just looking at it."

"That's what I was doin'. Lookin'." He turned the glass directly on Daphne. It gave her an odd feeling.

"Don't do that."

He giggled. "Funny."

She reached out and turned the glass aside. "Is that your father's glass?" When he nodded, she said, "He'll be mad you took it, won't he?"

"'E don't feel like chasin' me today."

"Why not?"

"'E don't feel good. 'E's got a black eye, 'e has."

"A black eye? Where did he get that?"

"Don't know." He gave her a slow wink. "Says he boomped into a door."

Daphne wondered if Mr. Randall drank. Somehow it was hard to imagine him in a brawl at a pub. "I've got to go," she said. "See you later. And quit spying on us." She ran across the meadow toward Aunt Daphne.

"Well," Aunt Daphne said as they walked back toward the car, "what did you think of the Randall hotel?"

"Weird," Daphne said. "It doesn't look like a real hotel."

"I understand it was quite popular in the days

75

when people took the train down from London and just stayed in one place and stared at the sea. Rocking chairs on the porch, you know, and cream teas at 5:00."

"Have the Randalls always owned it?"

"I believe so. They were apparently rather prosperous at one time. There are some very elegant Randall tombstones in the graveyards around here."

St. John laughed. "By their tombstones ye shall know them."

That explained for Daphne why Mr. Randall didn't have that humble quality she had noticed in Mrs. Jones. He had family pride to sustain him. She wondered how many generations that would last before reality set in. Her mother still talked about the estate in Somerset where her grandparents had lived, even though by the time she was grown up, the family fortunes had dwindled to a rather low level.

The path to the car angled so that they were actually closer to the Randall hotel, but the ground rose sharply, making it almost invisible except for two of the squat turrets and a portion of the thatched roof. Daphne looked that way to see if Nigel was still spying on them, but she couldn't see him anywhere.

Aunt Daphne reached the car just ahead of Daphne. She stopped short, with an exclamation that Daphne didn't catch.

"What is it?" St. John said. He caught up with her, and then he too stopped dead in his tracks. "By Jove!" he said in a strange tone of voice.

They were looking at something on the ground. Daphne peered over St. John's shoulder to see what it was. When she saw it, she felt the kind of numbing cold that she had felt before only when she walked into the frozen locker room at the ranch. Propped up against the side of the Mini was a wax figure, about a foot tall, of a woman. One leg was shorter than the other so that the figure tilted grotesquely, and a sharp bone dagger about the size of a big knitting needle pierced the hip of the shorter leg.

Aunt Daphne had turned white, but she tried to laugh as she bent down to pick it up. "My word!" she said shakily, "it's a jolly good likeness, isn't it?"

"Don't touch it!" St. John caught her arm. He picked up the figure himself, holding it with the tips of his fingers, and flung it off into the long grass. His face was stern, and for a moment Daphne could picture him in his army duty in Belfast. "Let's get out of here," he said. "Get in, Daphne—both of you. I'll drive."

No one spoke for several minutes. St. John turned the car around and drove fast up the narrow road, leaving the serene blue and green sea behind them.

"It's just nonsense, darling," Aunt Daphne said to him. "The Cornish adore that kind of thing. Don't let it upset you."

"It's a particularly nasty kind of nonsense," he

said. "I don't like it. Who do you think could have done it?"

"Old Mrs. Randall, I suppose, keeping in practice. Let's have a look at the Hardy church and then find a spot for lunch. We'll do the Stripple Stones tomorrow, if the weather holds."

Daphne kept thinking of Nigel and his spyglass. Could he have done this as a joke? But someone older than Nigel must have made the figure and thought of the cruel knife through the hip. She wondered if she should tell them about meeting Nigel, or for that matter of her own encounter with the old woman, but Aunt Daphne seemed to want to avoid the subject so Daphne said nothing. Perhaps later she could speak to St. John about it. She felt as he did, that there was something evil and menacing about that wax figure, although it seemed incredible that anyone could feel so hostile toward Aunt Daphne.

The feeling of foreboding stayed with her during their visit to St. Juliot's. It was a lovely little church in a quiet glen that seemed miles from anywhere, but it was eerie to know that it had originally been a chapel dedicated to a girl named Julitta, in the sixth century. Daphne felt as if she had walked into another dimension of time. She wandered down a grassy incline, through the graves, to a stile. Far across the fields was the roof of the vicarage where Hardy's future wife had grown up. Daphne traced the circular Celtic stone cross that stood near the stile and tried to imagine all these long ago people alive and laughing and talking. The silent graveyard gave back no echoes.

She shivered and went to rejoin Aunt Daphne and St. John. Further along the road they found a grassy place for lunch. Like most English people, Aunt Daphne kept small folding chairs in the car for picnics. It had amused Daphne at first to see people sitting by the road on chairs having a picnic, but then she had realized that much of the time the ground was too wet and muddy for sitting on.

It was a fine lunch, with wonderful small sandwiches with the crusts cut off and watercress on top. Aunt Daphne had a tiny spirit stove for making tea. Daphne smiled to herself, comparing this very civilized picnic with some of the campfire meals she had had in Wyoming, where everybody skewered chunks of steak on sharp sticks and cooked them over the fire, and baked potatoes in the hot ashes. Jake would have a pot of strong coffee boiling. For a moment she felt intensely homesick. But St. John, his worried look gone, was telling a funny story about a woman who wanted to find a painting that would match the mood she was usually in when she came to the breakfast room in the morning.

"Something black?" Aunt Daphne laughed.

"Something languorous, it seems. I thought an amusing Klee would be nice, but she didn't like that idea at all."

"Oh, I quite see that. It would be like having

someone there who insisted on telling rather subtle jokes. No, that wouldn't do at all."

Imitating the woman's affected accent, he said, " 'Something like a Monet, you know. Not too demanding. Something I can drift into.' "

"Ah! Not too demanding."

"I told her there wasn't anything 'like Monet' except Monet himself, and unfortunately we had no Monets for sale."

Daphne was glad St. John had come. Aunt Daphne seemed younger and gayer when he was there. By the time they got back to the cottage in midafternoon, the depressing effect of the wax figure seemed to have disappeared.

Aunt Daphne got out her key and they went in. She sniffed. "Oh, lovely. Mrs. Jones has been polishing the furniture. It was looking so dreary." She slipped off her coat and hung it on the coatrack. "Mrs. Jones is going to cook us a beautiful joint tonight, children. Mr. Alder saved it for us." She went on into the living room.

Daphne followed her aunt into the room, pulling herself together as she always did there to avoid knocking anything over. The room was so small, and there were so many of Aunt Daphne's little treasures.

Behind her, St. John said, "Hello! She's moved the painting."

Aunt Daphne gave a little start. "How very odd. She never touches my pictures. How very odd indeed." She turned to St. John, frowning. "I didn't move it, did I?"

"No. I took a last look at it as we left."

"Maybe when she polished the table," Daphne said. "She'd have to, wouldn't she?"

"It would be more like her just to work around it. Let's look for it." Aunt Daphne sounded urgent. "Daphne dear, will you take the bedrooms?" She hurried out of the room.

Daphne went up the stairs two at a time, bumping her head on the low ceiling. She went through all four bedrooms thoroughly but she could not find the painting. When she went downstairs again, Aunt Daphne and St. John stood in the hall looking bleak.

"No?" Aunt Daphne said to Daphne.

"Not a trace," Daphne said.

St. John groaned. He sank down onto a hall chair and stared at Aunt Dahne. "It's been stolen."

"It doesn't seem possible," Aunt Daphne said. "Who would even know about it?"

He shrugged and gave a sick little laugh. "Mrs. Jones?"

"That's out of the question."

"I know," he said. "It was just a feeble joke." He ran his hand over his face. "It wasn't insured, you see."

Aunt Daphne didn't say a word.

"Not insured?" Daphne said. "Isn't it quite valuable?"

"Quite," he said. "The man was coming from

Lloyd's on Monday to appraise it. I was mad to bring it here. I should have left it in the vault."

"My dear," Aunt Daphne said quickly, "don't blame yourself. I am as much to blame, leaving it in the house unattended. But who would have dreamed. . . ."

The sound of the back door opening made them all jump. Footsteps crossed the kitchen floor.

" 'Afternoon, all," said Mrs. Jones cheerily. "Have a lovely picnic, did you?"

11

Dear Bo:

It was like a scene from Agatha Christie. The unknown Turner painting that St. John had discovered and brought down to show Aunt Daphne BEFORE IT WAS INSURED had mysteriously disappeared while we were on a picnic. There were no signs of anyone being in the house except Mrs. Jones, who polished the table where the painting had been and who swears in a trembling voice that it was not there then, and she thought Aunt Daphne had put it away. Oh, and Mr. Randall, who came in to shake down the ashes and to have a cuppa with Mrs. Jones and to bang a few nails into the back stairs that he's been mending for weeks. Mr. Randall was wearing dark glasses, but otherwise was his usual self, Mrs. J. says, and they left the house together and she locked up as usual. But the painting is truly and incontrovertibly gone.

A constable from Camelford came to investigate. He is young and handsome and hails from Surrey, which Aunt Daphne says is a handicap because no one from across the Tamar River can really dig the Cornish. (She didn't say "dig.") For instance although he asked us many questions in a faintly stern and no nonsense manner, and also interrogated poor Mrs. Jones and Mr. Randall, later when St. John mentioned the wax figure that was left by the car out at the Strangles, the constable smiled indulgently, as if St. John were being fanciful. He said, "Oh, I don't believe you'll find any connection there, sir. These Cornish villages all have their odd old lady who likes to think she's a witch." He was very, very polite, but St. John thinks that he thinks there's something fishy about St. John's not having locked up the painting till it was insured. Aunt Daphne doesn't agree. She says what possible advantage could St. John gain in stealing his own painting? And St. John says, "But darling, it isn't my painting. It's gallery money, your money, friends and backers' money. Only some of it is my money. I could stash it away, you see, and sell it several years from now, and live on the Costa del Sol all my declining years." He jokes, but he's awfully upset. Poor little St. John.

And Mrs. Jones is sick with worry. She feels responsible somehow, although Aunt Daphne keeps telling her that's absurd. Mr. Randall hasn't been around much. He said, "You will have to excuse me, Mrs. Allerton-Kent. Constables annoy me. They're so bloody arrogant." But Constable Carter is not arrogant in the least. I think Mr. Randall just doesn't like to have to account to anyone for anything. I personally think he would be quite capable of stealing the painting, just to stir everybody up, but of course he didn't because he and Mrs. Jones left together. They alibi each other. Or do they?

It seems to me there are a lot of unanswered questions about Mr. Randall. Why, for one thing, does he hang around so much? I mentioned it, and St. John said he didn't trust him either, but Aunt Daphne thinks we're mistaking Cornish eccentricity for something more sinister. Maybe so. After all, what do I know about Englishmen?

Just before we left for the picnic, I ran back to get a bottle of ginger beer. I could have rushed the picture upstairs, hidden it, and disposed of it later . . . or left it in my room and sworn it wasn't there.

Your loving sister and number one suspect,
Daff

12

St. John called London and arranged with Malcolm, his assistant, to keep the gallery going by himself for a few days. St. John wanted to stay in Boscastle until the Turner was found. They all kept saying "until," as if there were no possibility of its not being found, but Daphne could see how worried they were.

Other men from the police department in Camelford came, asked questions, looked grave, and went away, but no one seemed to have any clues. Mrs. Jones, who was a nervous wreck about the disappearance, insisted on spending far more time at the cottage, as if to make up in work for what she seemed to feel was her irresponsibility. Aunt Daphne was unable to persuade her that no one blamed her for anything, so Mrs. Jones continued to hover, cleaning rooms that were already clean, polishing silver, cooking very good meals that usually they were too upset to appreciate.

Each coped with the disappearance of the picture in his own way. Aunt Daphne drove around the countryside, sometimes with Daphne, sometimes alone, stopping often to peer up and down hedge-rows. She had it in her mind that several years before some paintings had been stolen from a cottage in Week St. Mary, a little village up the coast, and had eventually been found abandoned in a ditch by a hedgerow. Those paintings too, she reminded St. John, had not been insured.

St. John spent a good deal of time wandering around town talking to people. By this time everyone knew that a painting had been stolen, although the police had advised playing down its value. He stopped in pubs, in shops, in the post office, wherever he could get into casual conversation with people. One thing he wanted to know was whether any strangers had been noticed around the village. No one seemed to know any more than Mrs. Jones, including Mr. Randall. There were still faint smudges of lavender and black under his eye, and he seemed a good deal more subdued than usual. He did his chores for Aunt Daphne and then left, not standing around in the kitchen with a cup of tea in his hand as he used to do. Daphne kept her eye on him. And so, she suspected, did Constable Carter.

One gray day Daphne walked out toward the Randall hotel, doing some snooping on her own. She wanted to talk to Nigel, whom she had hardly seen since the day at the Strangles.

It was easy enough to find him. He was lying on his back in the meadow, studying the clouds. He rolled over and eyed her warily. "Wot 'ee want?"

She sat down beside him on the cold ground. "That's not a very friendly greeting. I wondered what had happened to you. I haven't seen you."

"Nothin'. Here I am." He returned to his study of the sky.

"Aunt Daphne was telling me about puffins." When he didn't answer, she said, "You know, those funny birds that look like parrots. . . ."

"I know puffins," he said. "Wot about 'em?"

"She says they're hard to see. I thought maybe you'd know where I could see some."

"What for?"

"I like birds."

He thought this over for a moment. "Come on then." He jumped up and ran toward the cliffs. Daphne followed him, wondering if it was a wild goose chase . . . wild puffin chase? She really did want to see one of these strange-looking auks, but mostly she wanted to talk to Nigel. She had a feeling he knew things she'd be interested in hearing about. She hadn't forgotten the way he had watched Aunt Daphne and St. John with the spyglass, the day the wax figure had appeared and the painting had disappeared. Maybe, as the police said, there was no connection. But on the other hand, maybe there was.

She was breathing hard when she caught up with Nigel some distance up the coastline from the Randall hotel. He lay on his stomach and squirmed very cautiously toward the edge.

"Be careful!" Daphne said, remembering Aunt

Daphne's warning about crumbly cliffs.

Nigel shot her an amused look. "I been around these cliffs since I was born." He wriggled out a little further.

Daphne held her breath. She was sorry she had asked him about the puffins. When he gestured to her to join him, she shook her head.

"Scared, eh?" He grinned.

"Sure I'm scared. I don't want to break my neck. I'm not *that* interested in puffins."

He pointed to the cliff beneath him and said something she didn't understand. When she got him to repeat it slowly, she found he was saying that nesting puffins had dug out burrows along the cliff.

"Really? How do you know?"

"Seen 'er. She come out and walk on the beach with the myte, when the sun's going down."

"For real? You mean they stroll on the beach at sunset, like people?"

"Don't look like people."

She was intrigued. She came a little closer to the edge of the cliff and lay down in the stiff grass. She didn't dare go out far enough to see the burrow beneath them, but Nigel pointed out an old one further up the cliff. "How can a bird dig a hole in rock?"

"Uses her beak and shovels it out with her feet."

Daphne backed away from the cliff's edge. She wasn't sure whether Nigel was putting her on or not. "Maybe if we wait a while, we'll see one."

Nigel sat up, moved away from the edge, and

crossed his legs like a leprechaun, or, as the Cornish called them, "piskies." "Might. There's lots of 'em, but you got to know where to look."

She had noticed that sometimes his Cornish accent was so strong she could hardly understand him, but at other times it was much less noticeable. She wondered if he used it sometimes for effect.

It was cold on the cliff but she wanted to make him talk. She asked him questions about other birds, the terns and the different kinds of gulls, the shearwaters and the storm petrels. He knew a good deal about them although he didn't always know their names. He could tell her about their habits, their breeding grounds, their migration. He dropped his usual slightly mocking manner and talked seriously.

After quite a while she said suddenly, "Nigel, is your grandmother really a witch?"

He gave her a quick look, surprised at the change in subject. "Everybody knows that."

Trying to sound casual Daphne said, "Does she make wax figures of people and all that stuff?"

"Aye." His manner was more guarded now.

"Did she make a figure of my aunt? You know, that day you were watching us with the spyglass?"

He shrugged. "Don't know."

She tried a different tack. "Do you like my aunt?"

He nodded. "Gives me apples and bananas sometimes."

"Does your grandmother like her?"

He shrugged again. "She don't know her."

"Does your father like her?"

He made a face. " 'E don't like nobody." He jumped to his feet. "The puffin's noo comin' out." He ran off toward his house, and Daphne let him go.

All she had found out, other than the breeding and migrating habits of Cornish shore birds, was that Nigel's grandmother had probably made the wax figure of Aunt Daphne. But why? It didn't make any sense, unless it was done just for the sheer malicious pleasure of bedeviling a stranger. And as far as Daphne could see, it didn't have any connection with the theft of the painting.

She walked home slowly, trying to think what could possibly have happened to the painting. How had anyone gotten in, in broad daylight, and walked off with the painting, right there in the heart of town, seen by no one, leaving no trace? It didn't make sense. Unless Mr. Randall had stashed it away somewhere. But they had searched the house.

She stopped at the chemist's, remembering that Aunt Daphne wanted some aspirin. As she came out, the Englishman whom she thought of as the Major came along the street on his brisk walk. He touched his hat with his folded umbrella and said, "Lovely day." It wasn't, but Daphne had noticed the English said that unless there were an absolute downpour.

She agreed that it was a lovely day. The man fell into step with her as she walked toward the cottage.

"And how is your aunt enjoying her cottage?" he asked, in his cheerful, impersonal voice.

"Fine," Daphne said.

"Splendid. Does the ghost still rock the chair?" He smiled.

"I haven't actually seen it myself."

"Have you discovered the secret tunnel?"

Daphne looked at him. "Is there truly a secret tunnel?"

"Oh, they've always said so, you know. The cottage was owned by a wine merchant at one time, who became extraordinarily rich."

"Smuggling?"

He lifted his umbrella slightly. "One wouldn't wish to malign the dead, would one."

"I guess a lot of these places are supposed to have secret tunnels."

He nodded. "And probably do. Please remember me to your aunt, whom I have had the pleasure of meeting once or twice. Splendid woman." He touched his hat again and strode off up the hill.

Daphne went back to the chemist's shop and waited until the only customer had left.

"Forget something, dear?" the chemist asked her. He was a huge man, who made the small shop look even smaller.

"No, I wanted to ask you, Mr. Wilson, do you know who that man is who walks up and down the hill every day? He carries an umbrella and he looks like a retired army major or something."

"Oh, Colonel Featherstone," he said at once. "A fine man. Twice decorated, he was, in the war. Went out to India for a time, I believe."

"Is he Cornish?"

"No, he's from Dorset. Been here some time though."

She could tell he wondered why she asked, but she wasn't sure herself. "Thank you. I just wondered. I keep meeting him." She left the shop, thinking how close Colonel Featherstone came to fitting the background she had imagined for him. He hadn't mentioned the painting, which she was sure everyone in the village knew about by now. Perhaps he thought it was bad manners. She shook her head. It was hard enough trying to figure out who took the painting; it was complicated even further by not understanding what went on in English minds. She decided to do some more searching for a tunnel.

She came into the cottage and found Aunt Daphne and St. John standing in the living room examining a sheet of paper. She felt the electric tension at once. "What is it?" she asked.

St. John handed the paper to her. In lower case typewritten letters, unpunctuated, it said: "if you want picture come to tower of advent church at midnight tonight do not fail if you wish to see picture again do not call in police this is a warning."

"Where did it come from?" Daphne asked, puzzled.

"In the post."

"What are you going to do?"

Aunt Daphne turned the paper over slowly. "Go to Advent Church at midnight, I presume."

13

Mrs. Jones had agreed to spend the night in the cottage with her fifteen-year-old daughter, although Aunt Daphne had not explained to her why they would all be absent in the middle of the night.

"We have to go out," she had said, "rather late, actually, and it may be really quite late before we get home. I hate to leave the house empty now."

"Oh my, yes, yes indeed, you shouldn't leave it empty," Mrs. Jones had said, although it struck Daphne that she was nervous about staying.

She and her daughter were already in bed and presumably asleep in the second guest room when Daphne and Aunt Daphne and St. John left in the Mini for Advent Church. Advent was a tiny church on the moor outside Camelford. Aunt Daphne knew where it was, although she had not been there.

She drove up the dark narrow road toward Camelford. All three of them were quiet. St. John several times checked to make sure they had brought the three electric torches, and the pint of brandy that he had seemed to think they might need, and the chicken sandwiches Aunt Daphne had made. When Daphne had said, incredulously, "Chicken sandwiches?" Aunt Daphne had said, "My dear, there is no situation that a good chicken sandwich cannot improve. Who knows how long we will be gone?" Daphne had felt a chill along her spine. Aunt Daphne had tried, but not too hard, to persuade her to stay home, but Daphne would not hear of it. Stay home and miss everything? Certainly not.

Now, speeding along in the dark toward an entirely unknown situation in an eerie setting, Daphne thought of the sandwiches and felt a slightly hysterical giggle rise in her throat.

"What is it?" St. John said, hearing the catch in her breath.

"Nothing. It's just all so . . . so odd."

"It occurs to me," Aunt Daphne said, "that in your country, although you seem to have far more crime and violence than we do, it's rather more forthright. I mean, a bullet through the head, or a good honest strangling. Whereas in England even a petty thief has to deck out his deeds in witchcraft and mystery. If the person who stole the painting wants money for it, why couldn't he simply have said so? It's really very trying. Midnight in Advent Church, indeed!"

"You said 'witchcraft,'" Daphne said. "Then you do think there's a connection with the wax figure?"

"I shouldn't wonder," she said. "It's all so Cornish."

"We won't really find the painting at the church, will we?"

"I shouldn't think so. But we may find some kind of clue. The thieves who took the Week St. Mary paintings did all sorts of irrational things and finally abandoned them in a hedgerow."

St. John shivered. "Wrapped, I hope."

"Yes, actually. In plastic. It made no sense."

"I think you are being harassed," Daphne said. "Someone wants you to leave Cornwall."

"But why?" Aunt Daphne sounded hurt. "Surely I don't bother anyone."

"The chemist told me that the Cornish get mad because Londoners buy property and drive up the prices so the Cornish can't afford to live in their own villages any longer."

"But that's rubbish," Aunt Daphne said. "These towns would go under if it weren't for the visitors and the people who buy property." She shook her head. "As far as the Turner is concerned, someone knew it was there and knew its worth. I think it was stolen for money."

"But who could have known it was there?" St. John said, and then answering his own question: "I don't trust that bloody Randall."

"I suppose he is capable of a good deal," Aunt Daphne said, "but I really don't see him as a common thief."

Daphne didn't see him that way either, although she thought him capable of a good deal of villainy. It was all very puzzling.

The car wound along a darkened lane with high hedgerows on each side. Daphne had a vision of a whole coven of witches waiting to swoop down on them at Advent Church. What did witches do to you? She thought of the killing daggers in the museum. She would really hate to have her heart carved out on some lonely moor and pickled in a bottle. She shivered, and Aunt Daphne turned on the heater.

St. John had a thick sheaf of pound notes in his pocket that he had gotten at the bank in case the thief showed up and wanted to dicker. Now in an attempt to lighten the mood he sang a little tune, making it up as he went along. "I've got a packet in my pocket and I'm a long, long way from home." He made it sound like a cowboy song. Daphne giggled.

Aunt Daphne slowed down, peering off toward the open moor that rose on their right. She swung the car across the road into a lane just wide enough for the Mini, then drove in a short way until the lane ended at another hedgerow with a stile. She said, "I think this is it."

Daphne looked for the church and couldn't see a thing except the dark expanse of the moor that rose slightly under the dark sky. There was a heavy mist close to the ground.

Aunt Daphne slung her big canvas bag, which contained the chicken sandwiches among many other things, over her shoulder, and got her walking stick and a flashlight from the back seat. She gave Daphne another flashlight and St. John took the third and largest. Limping slightly Aunt Daphne walked resolutely up to the stile and climbed over. She had a moment of trouble getting her stiff leg over, but both Daphne and St. John knew better than to offer help. Aunt Daphne preferred to cope alone as much as possible. When she needed help, she asked for it.

Daphne followed her, and St. John came last. They set out across the moor, using their flashlights to keep from stumbling over rocks and brush. Somewhere in the gorse a nightjar sang. But the silence otherwise was so nearly complete, they might have been on some uninhabited planet. Daphne kept close to her aunt, who led the way slowly. Once Aunt Daphne stopped short, flashing her light down at an unusually green patch of moss.

"Bog moss," she said, taking a wide detour around it. "One can sink in. Rather unpleasant."

"Sometimes I realize," St. John said, "how ignorant we city people are. I thought that deep green was rather pretty. I'd have walked right into it."

But Daphne knew about sphagnum moss. Once she had rescued a colt who had stumbled into a bog and was sinking. She was glad Aunt Daphne was taking it slow and easy. It was very difficult to see the ground in all that mist. And she still could see no church. It was incredible to think that people crossed this stretch of moor to get to church. She asked about it, more to reassure herself with the sound of her own voice than anything else.

"There are only fifteen or twenty people who go

here," Aunt Daphne said. "I suppose most people go to St. Thomas à Becket in Camelford. Our poet laureate, Betjeman, has called Advent 'a sad little church.'" Again she stopped abruptly, and Daphne, stepping around her to avoid bumping into her, stumbled over something and fell to her knees. She gave a shriek. The thing she had stumbled against was alive and woolly. It gave a startled "baa" and trotted off into the mist. She had fallen over a sleeping lamb. The ewe, who had also been invisible, rose up and lumbered off after her lamb. Daphne got to her feet, shaking.

"Are you all right, love?" St. John helped her up. "What a terrifying thing."

"I'm all right," Daphne said. She felt foolish. That was the second time she had been frightened by a sheep, of all things.

"I'm sorry I didn't see them sooner," Aunt Daphne said. "Mind that rock they were sleeping against." She led the way around a granite boulder. "This stupid fog." In a moment she lifted her stick. "There is the church."

It took Daphne a moment to see it, and when she did make it out, it looked more like a shadow than anything as substantial as granite. It was small, and it had the usual Norman tower, but that was all she could see. It was separated from where they stood by a dip in the ground and a stream.

"How do we ford the stream?" St. John said. "Wade?"

"There's a stone bridge. Built by the Romans, actually. They used to come in here for tin." Aunt Daphne stood still a moment longer, studying the church. "We don't know what to expect, do we."

"I don't see any lights," Daphne said.

"I hear no welcoming brass bands," St. John said, but in spite of the attempt at a joke, his voice sounded tight. "No bagpipes."

"This may very well be a wild goose chase, of course," Aunt Daphne said. She looked at the other two. "I think our best strategy is to stick together, no matter what happens. I mean within touching distance. It is going to be very dark inside the church."

If this were only Wyoming, Daphne thought, at least one of us would have a gun. But that could lead to disaster, too. She followed as Aunt Daphne carefully picked her way down the steep footpath to the narrow stone bridge that suddenly loomed up in the mist. She could hear the soft whisper of the water. Across the river among the tipped and random gravestones of the churchyard, ghostly gray shapes stirred and moved, but Daphne kept her head this time. They were sheep, let in to graze on the grass there. Better than "eternal care," she thought, thinking of the sales pitch some of the cemeteries at home used. She followed Aunt Daphne across the sturdy bridge, trying to put her mind on the ancient Romans who had come this way, but she was unable to think of anything except what might be waiting for them in the church.

Single file and close together they climbed the

incline to the church. There was no sign or sound of anyone being about. Several times Aunt Daphne stopped and stood very still, listening.

When they reached the heavy oak door, she hesitated again, and then flashing her torch straight ahead, pushed at the door. It swung open in total silence—not a creak, not a scrape. As the three of them stood just inside on the cold stone floor, Aunt Daphne flashed her light toward the altar. The light lit up the simple gold cross for a moment and then Aunt Daphne swung around to the entrance to the tower.

The small beams of light from the flashlights seemed to get swallowed up in the total darkness inside the church. And the dark was reenforced by the cold, a damp penetrating cold that struck at one's bones. Daphne had the feeling that she would never be able to get that chill out of her body.

The tall, narrow, nail-studded door to the tower stuck. Aunt Daphne pulled and then St. John took over. It opened abruptly, nearly bowling him over. He flashed his light up the winding steps that were worn with age to a point where some of them offered little more than a toehold. At the very top of the tower, up where the bells were, there was a small wooden platform.

"That platform," St. John said, "is the only place in this tower that's big enough to hold the painting, if it were here." He sighed. "That means a scramble to the top."

"I'll go," Daphne said. "My arms are so long, I can reach up there without having to climb as high as you would."

"Be very careful," Aunt Daphne said. "One could have a very disagreeable fall."

Promising to be careful, Daphne started up the twisting steps, holding her flashlight in her left hand. After a moment she handed it down to St. John. "If you could keep your light beamed up here," she said, "that'd be great. I can't hang on to my light and climb, too."

Without the light it was a little easier, but the tower was so narrow she could just barely squeeze up the steps, and the steps were so small and so worn and so irregularly placed that several times she almost lost her footing.

"Don't stand right below me," she said. "If I fall, I'd land on top of you."

But St. John found that he had to stand just beneath her if he was going to light her way up.

"Do you see anything?" Aunt Daphne asked anxiously.

"Not yet." Their voice sounded hollow. Daphne clutched at a small ledge to keep her balance, but there was nothing on the ledge except dust that made her sneeze. The tower smelled musty. She began to feel claustrophobic, and fantasies of being trapped in this tower forever raced through her mind.

The higher she climbed, the more she had to let out her breath and squeeze past the tight turns. Suddenly something flapped past her face and she screamed.

"What is it? What is it?" Aunt Daphne's and St. John's voices were frightened.

"It's all right. I'm sorry. I think it was a bat. It flew out the window at the top of the tower. I'm sorry I scared you." She had always hated bats. She leaned back a little against the cold stones and craned her neck upward. There were three small windows, not much more than slits in the stone, but big enough for a bat to get out. She wiped her damp hands one by one on her jeans.

She reached up toward the platform, but she couldn't quite reach it. One more step, maybe. She wondered if there were more bats. And who knew what other horrors. She hated to touch the sides of the tower. The stones were clammy and cold. The bell ropes dangled in the center of the tower and she had to be careful not to get caught in them. She remembered Aunt Daphne saying that in the very old days these churches were sometimes used as forts and the tiny windows were places where people could watch and shoot at their enemies. It seemed like an odd function for a church.

She reached her long arm up again and touched the edge of the wooden platform. It was not much bigger than the missing painting, so if the painting were there, she would feel it at once. She reached around, her muscles stretching painfully. She

104

touched something cold. She didn't think it was the frame of the painting but she pulled it toward her and almost dropped it because it was heavier than she had expected. It was a broken stone fragment that must have been part of a font or some of the decoration in the church. In the pale light of St. John's flashlight she examined it. It was the head of an angel, exquisitely carved in stone. But it wasn't the painting. She put it back.

"There's nothing here except a stone angel."

"Come down then, dear," Aunt Daphne said. "Carefully."

Going down was even harder than going up because she had to dangle her foot until she found the step each time. The stone dust made her cough, and once she had to stop to get her breath. She longed for one deep lungful of Wyoming air.

Her foot slipped on slippery stone and she grabbed at the bell rope. Bells rang out wildly in the empty moor, their huge sound beating at Daphne in the tower. She tried to call out reassurance, but her voice was lost in the sound of the bells.

She came down the remaining steps as fast as she could, and caught the bell ropes, trying to stop the sound. St. John already had hold of them. In the light of Aunt Daphne's torch she could see the mixture of disappointment and laughter in St. John's face. Laughter won, and he leaned against the tower's stones clinging to the ropes.

"Will they come to church, do you think? those twenty people?" he said. "Oh, Daphne, love, you did give me a turn."

"I'm so sorry. My foot slipped, and I just grabbed at whatever was there."

"Not that one really believed the painting would be there," Aunt Daphne said, but she looked tired and disappointed.

Daphne felt angry at whoever it was that had sent them on this cruel chase.

"Couldn't be anywhere else, I suppose." St. John wandered down a side aisle, flashing his light into the pews.

Daphne turned toward the far side of the church to do the same. She flashed her light toward the outside corner of the front pews. She gasped and her flashlight fell to the floor with a clatter.

"What is it?" Aunt Daphne said. St. John hurried toward her, aiming his light. Daphne picked up her flashlight with shaking fingers and pointed it toward the end of the second pew, under a window. The figure of a man sat there.

14

"Oh, my word!" Aunt Daphne said.

"He isn't real," St. John said.

All three flashlights were aimed at the figure but for a moment none of them took a step toward him. It was a kind of scarecrow figure, wrapped in a rusty black cape with a wide turned-up collar. A broad-brimmed black hat was pulled down over the face.

With a sudden movement Aunt Daphne stepped forward and slashed at the head with her walking stick. It fell off and rolled across the stone floor.

"It's a soccer ball!" St. John said.

Daphne jumped to get out of the way of the gruesome-looking thing. She wouldn't have believed a soccer ball could be so macabre. It seemed to have some menacing life of its own.

Quickly and gingerly St. John dismantled the figure. When it lay on the floor in a bundle of old clothes, chicken wire, and padding, he said, "I thought there might be some clue."

"There is." Aunt Daphne picked up the dirty black hat and held it out to him on the end of her stick. Inside the brim a piece of cardboard was stuck, with words printed on it in black crayon.

He read them aloud. "Get out of Cornwall." He looked at her. "It doesn't make sense. Why does somebody want you to leave Cornwall?"

She shrugged. "I don't know, but I think they may get their way. I'm getting annoyed with all this."

"You can't just give up the cottage," Daphne said. "We'll fight them."

"One has trouble fighting an enemy one can't identify." Aunt Daphne began to gather up the pieces of the "man." "We mustn't leave this mess for the church people to deal with."

"We should give them to the police," St. John said, "and tell them what happened."

"Maybe they'll find fingerprints," Daphne said.

"Yes," St. John said. "Ours."

When they left the church, the sheep bunched together uneasily, watching them.

"We've ruined their night's sleep," St. John said.

When they got into the car, he brought out the brandy flask. "I for one could use a wee drop. Daphne?" He handed the flask to Aunt Daphne, who took a sip. "Young Daphne has earned her sip too, wouldn't you say?"

"Indeed yes," Aunt Daphne said. "And I think we had better have a chicken sandwich before we go."

Daphne felt the warm glow of the brandy in her throat and then in her stomach, and it dispelled some of the chill that she had thought would never leave her. And the chicken sandwiches were better than any she could ever remember eating. She looked out across the moor toward the invisible church. What a very strange experience! She would have to write Bo all about it. It was the kind of thing that would never happen in Wyoming.

When they got back to Bocastle, they found Mrs. Jones, fully dressed, sitting huddled by the electric fire, alone. She looked immensely relieved to see them.

"Whatever has happened?" Aunt Daphne said. "Why are you up? Where is your daughter?"

"Oh, she was that frightened, I had to call me husband to come and take her home."

"Frightened of what?"

"The noises. Down there." She pointed toward the cellar. "Thumps and scrapes and all kind of strange noises. She was sure it was the ghost. I told her there's no ghost here now. . . ." She looked at them uncertainly, as if for reassurance. "But she wouldn't hear of stayin' till morning. You know how children are . . . So as long as I had to get up, I thought I'd just get dressed, in case . . ." Her voice trailed off.

"I'm so sorry," Aunt Daphne said. "Mr. Everett will take you home. You won't mind, St. John?"

"Of course not. Just show me the way, Mrs. Jones."

When they had gone, Daphne said, "What do you think the Joneses heard?"

"Probably the echoes of their Cornish imaginations." But Aunt Daphne looked thoughtful. She bit absently into the last chicken sandwich, her head on one side as if she were listening.

"Do you think there really is a secret tunnel?"

"No. I've poked about a bit and I couldn't find one."

"I have, too." Daphne told her about the night when Mr. Randall surprised her in the cellar.

Aunt Daphne frowned. "I really don't like the way he roams about the house whenever he chooses. I must speak to him about it."

"I don't know how he got into the cellar without my hearing the door squeak."

"I suppose . . . sometimes if you lift a door a little when you open it, it doesn't squeak. He may have learned that. But I don't like his being there. I shall tell Constable Carter about this."

"Maybe you should get his key from him, the key to this house, I mean, so he can't come and go when he wants."

Aunt Daphne gave her a strange look. "He doesn't have a key." Then she gave herself a little shake. "Mrs. Jones must have let him in, or lent him her key. I'll speak to her. My dear, we must watch our own imaginations, or we'll be thinking next that Mr. Randall is the ghost of our nineteenth-century smuggler. Go to bed now. You must be very tired. Sleep late in the morning."

15

Dear Bo:

I'll take up where I left off in yesterday's letter. St. John and Aunt Daphne did have a long talk with the constable, and I think he was "vexed," as Aunt Daphne calls it, because we went out to Advent without telling him. But he is much too polite to say so. The English are so polite to each other, it's amazing they ever get anything done. Not that I think they should be rude, but I mean, it's hard to figure out what they really think. It is for me anyway. Probably they understand each other. But for instance, if I were Aunt Daphne, I'd have a few hundred questions to ask Mr. Randall. Starting with why hasn't he been around to take in the dustbins. St. John and I hassled them in this morning because Aunt Daphne's aesthetic sense was suffering. I have a feeling Mr. Randall knows a lot about everything that goes on. But Aunt Daphne says you can't just ask a person rude questions. It wouldn't be polite. See what I mean?

St. John had to drive up to London today to see

to the gallery, but he'll be back Friday. He is worried sick about the missing painting. I wish I could surprise him by finding it. I really think I have a thing about St. John, except that he's about a foot shorter than I am (not really, but quite a few inches). We look like Oley Olson and Stalky in "Steve Canyon." Besides, he thinks I'm a child. A nice child but still a child. I wish I could skip about five years and lop off five inches.

I loved your long letter and I'm glad you're on the dean's list. When do you start making violins? Do many people buy violins? I guess that's a stupid question. I can't imagine Stradivarius asking that question.

Love,
Sis

16

Daphne couldn't believe it when Mr. Randall came back to do the chores and Aunt Daphne didn't even ask where he had been.

"Good morning, Mr. Randall," she said.

"Good morning, madam," he said. As if he hadn't been away at all. As if nothing at all had happened. He didn't even ask if they had found the painting. But of course he probably knew they had not because there had been a news item on the nationwide TV show the night before. Aunt Daphne didn't have a television, but Mrs. Jones told them about it.

"He spoke of that theft in Week St. Mary a few years ago, you remember, madam?"

Aunt Daphne remembered.

"And that girl that stole the paintings from her own father, and then the lot in Ireland, you know, that she picked out for the IRA. What was her name?"

"Rose Dugdale."

"That's the one. You don't think Rose Dugdale is behind our problem, do you, madam?"

"I think she is still in prison, Mrs. Jones. And I am sure she would not be much interested in our little Turner. She was interested in helping the IRA."

"Not Irish, is she, madam?"

"No, English. Devon, as I recall, or perhaps Dorset."

Mrs. Jones guided her iron expertly down a sleeve of one of Daphne's shirts. "Well, people are that peculiar."

Daphne heard her talking to Mr. Randall later in the kitchen when he came up for his tea break. Aunt Daphne had gone upstairs to work. Daphne wandered into the kitchen and let Mrs. Jones fix her a cup of tea. She noticed that Mr. Randall's eye still had a faint lavender blotch around it.

"We've missed you, Mr. Randall," she said. Aunt Daphne would have frowned disapprovingly at this line of attack, but Aunt Daphne wasn't there.

Mr. Randall glanced at her sideways with his hard, bright eyes. "Always glad to be missed."

Not much progress there. She decided to plunge. "Were you ill?"

He looked amused. "No, no trouble there."

She saw that that was all the information she was going to get: he had not been sick, period. She had been told, by implication, to mind her own business. She finished her tea and went outdoors. The sky was cloudy but there was a hint of spring mildness in the air. She decided to walk down to the jetty to see if the little gift shop that sold secondhand books had opened for the season yet.

It had not opened, nor had any of the other shops. She stood with her face to the window trying to see some of the titles. The people who owned these shops that opened only in the season seemed to have walked out and locked the door on the last day of business, leaving everything where it had been. In America, she thought, they'd be robbed blind before spring came around again. But here no one seemed to bother.

She crossed over the little stone-arched bridge and reread its inscription that said it belonged to the lord of the manor. On the other side she sat down on a warm rock and looked at the boats, heeled over now at low tide. She picked out the faded blue fishing boat that belonged to Mr. Randall. It was called the *Viking*, which seemed rather a presumptuous name for such a modest-appearing boat. She wondered if Mr. Randall thought of himself as a descendant of Vikings. It struck her as a funny idea, and she laughed aloud. A gull who had been sitting on the edge of the jetty flapped his wings as if he were about to take off, but then thought better of it.

A voice behind her startled her. "That's me dad's boat." It was Nigel, who stood looking down at her. "Like me dad's boat?"

"I don't know anything about boats," she said. "You scared me."

He laughed. And then as a car came slowly down

the narrow road, his expression changed to alarm. "Hide me! Quick!" He ducked behind her.

She moved to conceal him as the car slowed and turned toward the bridge. The middle-aged man at the wheel nodded pleasantly and said, "'Morning."

She said good morning and watched him drive across the bridge and up toward the village on the other side of the jetty. "He's gone," she said to Nigel.

"Whew! That were a close'un!" He stood up, brushing off the ragged knees of his trousers.

"Who was it?"

"That were Sir."

"Sir?" She was puzzled.

"Yeah, Sir. 'E's out lookin' around for kids that don't come. Like me."

"Is he a teacher?"

"No, he's Sir."

"The principal?"

Disgusted with her ignorance, he said slowly and distinctly, "Sir. Headmaster."

"Oh. We call ours the principal."

"Don't know no principal. 'E's just Sir. Miss probably got 'im after me. Miss gets in a state when I don't come. Sir came to see me dad but me dad throwed him out."

"You ought to go to school."

He made a face. "You ain't in school."

"Well, I . . ." It was too long and incomprehensible a story to tell Nigel. "I'm visiting my aunt."

"I'm visitin' me mum." He laughed at his joke.

"Does your father take his boat out much?" Daphne asked. "Do you ever go with him?"

"Used to. Now he only goes out at night."

"Oh? What kind of fish does he catch at night?"

The laughter died out of his face and he began to edge away. "He don't catch fish."

Daphne was surprised and instantly curious. Why would a man brave those dangerous, unpredictable seas if not for something profitable, like fish? And especially at night.

"'E don't tell me nothin'."

Daphne walked along with him. "I'll bet you get curious though." When he didn't answer, she said, "Isn't it dangerous out there at night?"

"Me mum gets scared. She wants him to quit it, but they won't let 'im."

"Who won't?"

He made a vague gesture. "Them."

Daphne felt a prickle of excitement. Was she learning something? "Was it 'them' that gave him the black eye?" she said, trying to sound casual.

"'E ain't saying." He looked at her. "Me nanny fixed it so he won't drown."

"How did she do that?"

He pointed back to the boat. "Nailed a horseshoe to the bottom of t'boat."

"That does it?"

"Everybody knows that. Don't tell Sir y' seen me." He ran away before she could answer.

She looked back at the Randall boat. Up in the

bow end, alongside the keel, she could see part of a rusty horseshoe.

Whatever it all meant, if anything, was more than she could figure out.

At the other end of the jetty she came upon Constable Carter, the policeman who had first come to investigate the theft of the painting. He had his hands clasped behind his back, and the chinstrap of his tall helmet made him tilt his head forward a little. He smiled and nodded. "'Morning, miss."

"Good morning." She wondered how long he had been watching her. Did he just happen to show up or was he investigating? They were all so casual and offhand, you couldn't tell. "I was just looking at Mr. Randall's boat," she said, to see if she would get a reaction.

"Ah?" He raised his eyebrows slightly, making his helmet shift. His face had no expression.

"Yes. It seems like such a little boat to go out in at night in those rough seas."

"Boscastle men are accustomed to the sea."

Exasperated, she nodded, returned his vague smile, and walked on up the street. When it came to figuring out the English, she was a failure.

17

Daphne missed St. John. She would be glad when Friday came and he was back. Meanwhile he called to see if there was any news. On Thursday just before dinner Daphne was riveted to attention when she heard what her aunt was saying on the phone.

Her voice was low, and Daphne hoped it was because she didn't want Mrs. Jones to hear, not because she wanted to exclude Daphne. In any case Daphne's curiosity was so great, she found herself quite unable to move out of earshot like a tactful and honorable niece. She went on reading Graham Greene and listening with all her might.

"I've just had another note," Aunt Daphne was saying. "It must have slipped to the floor when Mrs. Jones brought in the post. I didn't see it until a few minutes ago." Pause. "Yes, same sort of thing, only this time it's the Trethevy Quoit. . . . Well, my dear, it's a megalithic burial mound. And Trethevy is a splendid example. Our friend has good taste in archaeology." She paused. "Also it's a goodish distance from here. . . . Yes, I agree. Saturday is the day mentioned, no hour this time."

Daphne couldn't believe it. They weren't going to fall for that futile chase again, were they? She strained forward to hear Aunt Daphne.

"If it's a nice day," Aunt Daphne was saying, "we may as well take a picnic and enjoy the moor. I want to show Daphne the Davidstow air field. Her father was stationed there during the war . . . Yes, well, try not to worry, my dear. I'm sure it will all come out well in the end. Keep the faith. . . . Drive carefully on the way down. . . . Good night, St. John."

Daphne gave her whole attention to Graham Greene as Aunt Daphne came in from the hall.

"You heard me, I suppose, my dear?"

Feeling guilty, Daphne nodded. "I couldn't help . . ." She broke off. You didn't indulge in even half a lie when Aunt Daphne was giving you that direct look.

"Of course. I want you to know." She handed Daphne a typed letter that looked like the first one, no punctuation, no capital letters: "the first time was to test you come as before with no word to anyone else trethevy quoit saturday."

"Isn't he just leading us down the garden path?" Daphne said. She couldn't bear to see her aunt made a fool of. When Aunt Daphne looked puzzled at the expression, she said, "I mean, isn't he putting us on? You know, leading us a merry chase?" "Without doubt. I shall discuss it with Constable Carter. Someone, I think, wants us away from the cottage." She turned away as Mrs. Jones came into the hall. "Mrs. Jones, you mustn't stay so late. Your family needs you."

"Just leaving, madam. I wanted to tell you the lamb is cooking up to a nice crisp. It should be ready in about ten minutes by my reckoning."

"Splendid," Aunt Daphne said. "Let me get my checkbook and give you the week's pay." Mrs. Jones liked to be paid on Thursdays so she could buy "a nice bit of fish" from the fish truck.

When Mrs. Jones had collected her check and gone home, Daphne helped her aunt get the dinner on the table. As usual, in Daphne's opinion, the meat was delicious and the vegetables were awful. The English seemed unable to get out of a peas-brussels sprouts-cauliflower rut, and Daphne was heartily sick of them all. But there were Mrs. Jones's wonderful rolls and good Cornish butter, and a trifle for dessert. She had the pleasant feeling of being well-fed, and she was relieved that she had made it through the meal with no greater disaster than dropping a buttered roll, buttered side down of course, on Aunt Daphne's hand-hooked rug. Maybe someday coordination would set in and she would be as deft and controlled as Aunt Daphne. But she doubted it.

Aunt Daphne excused herself to do some work on her book. It was a mild evening with only a light breeze. Daphne decided to take a short walk before she settled down for the night. She didn't want to disturb Aunt Daphne to tell her where she was going so she let herself out of the house quietly. She wouldn't be gone long.

She walked down the hill toward the harbor. The evening sky was a soft luminous gray, the evening star hanging low. Cornwall was really beautiful when it stopped knocking you down with its wind and its rain long enough so you could get a look. The village was already tucked up for the night, although it was not yet nine o'clock. Single lights burned in cottages, and Daphne thought of the wasteful blaze of electricity in houses at home. Streetlights here were spaced far apart and she had discovered that they went off at midnight. When she had mentioned that to Mrs. Jones, the answer had been, "Repectable people should be at home long before midnight."

The shops had closed and even the petrol station was dark. There was no one on the street. Daphne hesitated, wondering if she should go back. But since she was out, she decided to walk down to the jetty. It was such a lovely night. Over her head the stars were appearing as the darkness deepened. The tide was in, and the boats anchored off the jetty bobbed gently.

Daphne leaned on the stone bridge and looked down the water toward the outer bar, an eighteenth-century sea wall that had been partly destroyed by a mine in World War II and then rebuilt by the National Trust. Off to her left, out of sight now in

the darkness, was Forrabury Church, where Aunt Daphne had taken her one afternoon to see the six-foot-tall Greek stone cross, one of the oldest in Cornwall.

She left the bridge and climbed the hill. From the top she could just see the outer curve of a small cove. As she looked down, she was startled to see a boat wing around the promontory and into the cove. It had one small light in the bow. She heard the low throb of the engine and then it was cut off. The dark figures of two men rose up in the bow, a third in the stern. The boat grated against the sand and one of the men jumped out.

They were unloading something. At first she assumed it was fish, but then she saw it was a stack of long boxes that they piled up on the sand. She moved a little closer so she could see better, but the gravel scattered under her foot and some pebbles fell down the side of the cliff. She ducked back, out of sight.

She couldn't imagine why they would be unloading anything in that cove, which was flooded at high water. Getting boxes of that size up to the top of the cliff would be impossible unless they had a winch or something. It was all very peculiar.

It seemed to her that the boat had looked like the *Viking*, but she wasn't sure at all. Those little boats looked a lot alike.

She waited about ten or fifteen minutes, until she heard the boat's engine again. She edged near enough to see it as it disappeared. There was no sign of anything on the beach. She wished she could climb down and examine the beach, but she knew that was too dangerous. The tide was already turning. She started toward home.

She walked quickly up the hill. Just before she reached Aunt Daphne's cottage, she heard footsteps behind her. Her impulse was to run, but that seemed foolish. What was she afraid of? She made herself slow down and turn around.

It was Colonel Featherstone, out for one of his strolls, tap-tapping his walking stick as he came up the hill. He stopped when he caught up with her. "Good evening, young lady." His dog sniffed at Daphne's knees.

"Good evening, Colonel," she said. She felt limp with relief. "You startled me."

"Oh, I'm so sorry. Terribly sorry."

"That's all right. It's just that hardly anyone is out." She scratched the dog's ears. He was a nice dog.

"True. Our little village is a quiet place at night." He looked back down the hill. "Usually very quiet indeed."

"I was watching a boat come in," Daphne said.

"Yes, I too."

"Really?" It startled her that she hadn't seen him. She wondered where he had been standing.

"I have a shocking curiosity." He smiled at her.

She laughed. "I have, too."

"I have observed that." He touched his hat with his stick. "Good evening."

She watched him go up the hill. When she went into the house, Aunt Daphne stood in the hall with her coat on.

"My dear!" Aunt Daphne said. "I couldn't think where you had gone."

"I'm sorry. Did I worry you?"

"I'm afraid you did a bit. Such odd things seem to be happening these days."

Daphne saw herself kidnapped. "Allerton-Kent American niece disappears." "I'm sorry. I wanted some fresh air and I hated to disturb you. I met Colonel Featherstone just now. He's a strange little man, isn't he."

"Is he? He seems to me quite the usual English-man. Quite nice actually."

"Oh, very nice. I didn't mean that." She hoped she hadn't offended Aunt Daphne.

"You meant English, perhaps. I'm sure your Wyoming cowboys would seem strange to me. Shall we have a cup of tea before bed?"

As they drank their tea, Daphne told her aunt about the boat. "It looked like Mr. Randall's."

Aunt Daphne was quiet for a few minutes. "He's always been involved in what he calls his enterprises. I understand some of them have interested the police. Constable Carter told me they pay his old hotel a surprise visit every now and again."

"What could they have been doing in that cove?"

"I don't know, dear. We'll mention it to the constable. But I do wish, dear Daphne, that you wouldn't be quite so adventurous, especially at night. Something could happen to you, you know."

"I'm sorry. I'll be more careful."

After she had gone to bed, she lay awake trying to think what people would be smuggling. Drugs wouldn't come in big wooden boxes. And it was interesting that Colonel Featherstone had turned up on the scene.

18

Dear Bo:

It's Saturday morning very early, before anyone is awake. I didn't sleep much last night. I'll tell you what happened. First, St. John arrived last evening. He was depressed to hear we had no new news about the painting, but he's trying to believe it might be at Trethevy Quoit, though why either of them think it will be, I can't imagine. They were fooled once, and they'll be fooled again. In my opinion someone is just trying to get Aunt Daphne so bugged and upset she'll leave town. If I could only figure out who would gain by her going, but I can't. Mr. Randall, for instance, would lose some income. Ditto for Mrs. Jones, though no one suspects her of anything any-way. But I'm like Miss Marple in Agatha Christie—everybody is guilty till proven innocent. Of course the theft of the painting may be totally unrelated to the little witchcraft dealies, but it does seem like an odd coincidence. Last night before we went to bed, Aunt Daphne stepped outside for a breath of air and there was a bottle on the step with a pickled leg of a frog in it. We all felt so sick, we had to sit up another hour and drink tea and console each other. This witch stuff is really nasty. St. John took it and locked it up in his car and he's going to show it to Constable Carter this morning. Although Con. C. doesn't seem to think there's any connection.

Well, let me get on to the main event. I was just dozing off when I heard this muffled thumping noise. It seemed to come from the cellar, but I couldn't be sure. I remembered the noises Mrs. Jones and her daughter heard, that Aunt D. said were Cornish imagination. I thought maybe I was hallucinating too (or is that just visual?). Anyway I tried to tell myself I'd been dreaming, but the noise came again a little louder. I was scared stiff, but I couldn't just lie there and quake. So I put on my robe and got my flashlight and crept down the stairs into the kitchen. I had just started to open the cellar door when I heard a rustle behind me and I NEARLY FAINTED!! But it was St. John, and he was terribly apologetic about scaring me. He'd heard the noise too, and he was investigating, and I guess I scared him as well. We had a council of war and decided we'd both go down into the cellar and investigate. By now the noise had stopped, and we told ourselves it might be the cat from across the street, who does get in from time to time and chases mice. Well, we snuck down the cellar stairs very quietly with our lights out (I almost ruined the descent by tripping on the second step but St. John caught me.) It was completely dark down in the cellar, like being in a cave, which is really kind of what it is because the house is built against the side of a hill, you see. You couldn't hear a thing. Then I bumped into a barrel and knocked off some glass fruit jars. You could hear that all right. St. John switched on his light very fast and swept it all around the cellar, in the old coal bins and the woodpile and the new closet Mr. Randall has been working on for Aunt Daphne to keep jars of preserves in. (She never preserves anything actually but Mrs. Jones likes to.) Nothing was there, not even the cat. St. John switched on the light bulb that hangs from the ceiling, and we did another thorough hunt, not really knowing what we were looking for, although I for one had that darned secret tunnel in my mind.

By this time of course Aunt Daphne had heard us and had come down to see what was going on. In her opinion it was the cat who had probably come in and gone out again. She pointed out the broken pane of glass in the window at ground level. She said Mr. Randall never seemed to get around to fixing it, although he was so hot for fixing other things.

St. John was examining the big wooden closet or cupboard thing that Mr. R. had been building. He was right inside it looking at the back, and suddenly he said, "I say!" I think that's one of the weirder English expressions. I always want to say "you say what?" Anyhow we said what it is, and he said, "I say! Come have a look." Needless to say, we did.

And Bo, you won't believe what he'd found. If you turned a certain couple of screws and took them out, the back of the cupboard swung out like a door! He'd discovered it because it had little hinges at the side, and he couldn't understand why it would have hinges if it wasn't supposed to open.

On the other side of the door . . . brace yourself! . . . was a tunnel. I was so excited, I was almost sick. It was a small tunnel, only big enough for midgets, or for crawling in. It had obviously been there a long time, but St. John pointed out where there had been dirt dug recently, and there were some shiny new nails in the beams that held up the tunnel. St. John had to scrunch down to get through the tunnel and I had to go on my stomach. Aunt Daphne stayed in the cellar. Well, it was pretty uncomfortable, with dirt in one's face and cobwebs and really cold, but we were too excited to mind much. However, it came to a sudden end. Instead of coming out at the harbor or some exciting far-off place, we came out after a few yards in the potting shed. Up through a trapdoor in the floor. Let me explain, the potting shed is built right up against the side of the hill, like an old Wyoming sod hut. It's kind of big, as such things go, and of course it's full of pots, mostly empty, and sacks of things like fertilizer and potash and what not, and Aunt Daphne's huge gardening bonnet hanging on a nail. It was such an anticlimax, coming up through the floor into that domestic, homey-looking shed. We were so disappointed that the tunnel ended there. We couldn't figure it out. Did the wine merchant stash illegal booze in his potting shed? It didn't make sense. Anyway there's nothing illegal there now. We practically took the place apart to make sure there was no painting hidden there, or anything else that shouldn't be. Then we went back through the garden to tell Aunt Daphne, who was beside herself wanting to know what we'd found. St. John and I got thoroughly brushed off in the cleaning-up room and we all had a cup of tea and tried to figure out not only why the wine merchant had built that short, ridiculous tunnel, but why Mr. Randall was fooling around with it.

"The only way to find out," St. John said finally, "is to ask him. Before we go out to the moor tomorrow, I shall have a little talk with Randall." He promised I could go with him, to show him where the Randalls live. So here I am, waiting very impatiently for him to get up so we can have breakfast and go out there. I think I hear him in the shower, so I'll close for now and give you the next installment later. Remember when I thought Cornwall would be dull?

Love,
Daff

p.s.: We still don't know what the noise was that we all heard.

19

While Aunt Daphne and Mrs. Jones made the picnic lunch, Daphne went with St. John, first to Camelford to report the latest developments to the constable and to give him the "witch gift," as St. John called it; and then to find Mr. Randall.

St. John said, "I'll be right back," at the police station, leaving Daphne in the car. Actually it was fifteen minutes before he returned. "I'm sorry, love," he said. "I didn't mean to desert you. Constable Carter was feeling chatty."

"Does he think we should go to that Quoit place?" Daphne was sure the constable would have more sense.

"Oh, yes. He wants to see who comes around while we're gone. Now then, how do we get to the Randall hotel?"

As they drove out toward the Randalls', Daphne kept silent except for giving directions. She was a little bit miffed because St. John had not taken her into the police station with him, and she wondered if he were keeping anything from her. Also he himself seemed unusually quiet and thoughtful, and she didn't like to interrupt his thinking.

When he parked a little distance from the Randall place, she waited, not knowing whether he wanted her to come.

"Oh, do come with me," he said. He ran around the car and opened the door for her. "I didn't mean to be beastly at the police station. I'm so sorry."

He gave her such an engaging smile, she forgave him instantly. And her morning was made still more pleasant by the discovery of half a dozen new-born lambs, who peered at her shyly from the protection of their mother's flanks.

"Oh, look, aren't they cute," she said.

St. John smiled and agreed, but she remembered he was not an animal enthusiast. She felt sorry for people who grew up in the city.

"I'm glad it's April," she said.

" 'Oh, to be in England?' "

She pointed ahead to the just-visible thatched roof of the hotel. "There it is." It looked forbidding in the gray morning mist.

"Right-o. I hope our friend is at home."

It seemed odd to her that they were tracking down Mr. Randall. At home the police would have gone out to question him about the tunnel, wouldn't they?

There was no sign of life as they came up to the untidy back entrance. St. John made a face as they followed the dirt path through an assortment of over-flowing trash cans. He had brought his umbrella tucked under his arm, and now he raised it and rapped sharply on the door with the handle.

Nothing happened. He rapped again and called out loudly: "Anyone about?"

After a few minutes a second floor window was flung open and the ragged gray head of Nigel's grandmother appeared. She screamed something at them in a Cornish accent that neither of them understood.

"I say, is Randall about?" St. John called up to her.

She slammed the window shut and disappeared.

"A real charmer," St. John muttered. He knocked again, imperiously.

"Shall I go around to the front and see if I can find Nigel?" Daphne asked.

"Better stick together," St. John said. "I don't want the old hag tossing you over the cliff." He knocked again.

The door opened suddenly and Nigel's mother stood there, her cotton-candy hair done up in huge curlers. She looked half-frightened, half-defiant, and her green eyes stared at them in the same penetrating way that Daphne had noticed when she first saw her. "Wot ye want?" she said in a low voice.

"Randall, if you please," St. John said. He was not as brusque as he had been with the old woman.

"Not t' home," she said, starting to shut the door.

St. John caught at the door. He looked suddenly

angry. "You tell him for me, please, that I want to talk to him."

"I told you, 'e's not home." She tugged at the door and now she did look plainly frightened.

"When do you expect him then?"

"I don't know, I truly don't."

"Not skipped out, I hope?"

"I got no idea where he is, I'm sure."

St. John still held the door. "You tell him, if you please, that I want to see him. I am a guest at Mrs. Allerton-Kent's cottage."

"Yes, I know, sir."

"Very well. I would like to see him either this morning or in the evening after 7:00. I shall be away in the afternoon. No one will be there in the afternoon, you understand?"

"Yes, sir."

He released the door. "I shall expect him."

When they were out of earshot, Daphne said, "Do you think he was there?"

"Haven't the foggiest." He seemed cheerful now. He slashed at the long grass with his umbrella and laughed when a startled lamb some distance away baa'ed. "Sorry, love."

"If Mr. Randall knows we're going to be away, he might come poking around," Dahpne said.

"He might indeed," St. John said.

"Oh, I see." Daphne felt stupid. He had done that on purpose. He and the constable had laid a trap. She shouldn't be so quick to think people weren't as smart as she was.

Just before they got to the car, there was a low whistle behind them. Nigel materialized from the hedgerow. He looked back to make sure no one at the hotel could see him.

"You lookin' for me dad?" he said. His usual mischievous gleam was gone.

"Yes, Nigel," Daphne said. "Mr. Everett wants to talk to him. Do you know where he is?"

"Ain't home."

"We know that," St. John said, but Daphne cut in quickly, afraid Nigel would take offense and leave.

"Where is he?" She waited. "We have to talk to him."

"They got 'im."

"Who?" It was the mysterious "they" again.

He jerked his head toward the general direction of the sea. "Them."

"Look here," St. John began.

Daphne interrupted him again. "Is somebody hurting him, Nigel? Are you worried?"

"Ay. They's tough. They hit 'im."

"What for?"

Nigel shrugged. " 'E don't tell me nothin'."

"Do you want us to tell the police?"

He looked frightened. "No, no, no. Don't do it."

"All right, but if you find out where he is, will you let me know?"

He glanced briefly at St. John, hesitated, and nodded.

"We'll be gone until evening, but you could leave me a note. Stick it in the mailbox."

His old grin returned for a moment. "Can't write."

"Oh, you can write a little. Or just draw a picture." She pulled a pencil from her pocket and found a scrap of paper in the car. She drew a round smiling face and gave it to him. "Just draw me one of those. I'll know you want to see me."

He took it, nodded, and ran.

St. John called after him. "I say . . ." but it was in vain. He looked exasperated. "We could have got something out of him. I know about kids like him—I was one myself. Tough kids. You have to be tough with them."

She shook her head. "That wouldn't work with Nigel. He only told me because I'm his friend and he's worried about his father."

"Probably all a neat little plot," St. John said, opening the door for her. "Probably the father told him to say that, to put us off the track."

Daphne made an effort to keep her patience. She didn't want to get cross with St. John, of all people. After all, he didn't know Nigel. She told him about seeing the boat unloaded, and he was instantly interested. Then she mentioned the Irishman who had come to the back door looking for Mr. Randall.

"Irishman! Did anybody ever tell Daphne or Constable Carter?"

Daphne was startled. It hadn't impressed her

especially, and she had not thought to tell her aunt. "Maybe Mrs. Jones did."

"You can jolly well bet she didn't. They hang together, the whole lot."

"What lot?"

He made an impatient gesture. "Country people." He drove in silence for a few minutes, frowning and thinking. "A boat. An Irishman. Boxes. A tunnel that doesn't go anywhere. Randall's black eye. A missing painting. The effort to get Daphne to sell the house. What does it all add up to?"

"If I knew . . ." Daphne began.

He gave her a quick smile. "Just a rhetorical question, love. Forgive me if I'm jumpy. I'm so worried about the bloody painting." Again he was silent. "Not Catholic, is he? Randall?"

She was surprised at the question. "Catholic? No, I don't think so. I'm sure he isn't. Mrs. Jones refers to the Randalls as 'chapel . . .'"

"Not Catholic then. I was just thinking if he was, maybe the IRA . . ." He shook his head. "But it doesn't fit, does it. Unless . . ."

"Unless what?" She couldn't resist asking.

"Got to think about it a bit."

"Colonel Featherstone is curious, too. He saw the boat unload."

"Who's he?" When she told him, he said, "Oh yes. Talked to him in the pub, I think. Proper little military type."

"He's very nice." She didn't know why she felt

she had to defend Boscastle people. It had never occurred to her before that she thought much of them one way or the other.

"Retired sort. Got to keep his interest up through nosing around the local affairs, I shouldn't wonder. No problem there."

"No, I hadn't meant he was a problem. Just that he might have some ideas. . . ."

"Perhaps we'll catch up with him," he said vaguely, "one of these days." He parked the MGB in front of the cottage, and they went in to report to Aunt Daphne.

But Mrs. Jones was still there, so St. John simply shook his head.

"Mrs. Jones has fixed a splendid lunch," Aunt Daphne said. "Pasties and all sorts of goodies."

"Marvelous," St. John said. "I've never had a pasty in my life."

"Oh, my word," Aunt Daphne said, smiling. "A life wasted."

"I'll just get that jar of spiced peaches to top things off, madam." Mrs. Jones started for the cellar stairs.

Daphne saw St. John signal wildly to Aunt Daphne just as it popped into her own mind that they had not gone back to the cellar last night to put the cupboard door back in place. They had come in through the garden and the kitchen door.

With completely unflurried smoothness Aunt Daphne got to the cellar door before Mrs. Jones did.

"Not now, I think, Mrs. Jones. We'll save them for dinner. The syrup attracts the bees so, and Miss Daphne is allergic to bee sting."

Daphne swallowed. "Oh, terribly," she said, crossing her fingers inside her pocket. "Practically fatal."

"Oh, what a pity. Well, if you do get stung, Miss Daphne," Mrs. Jones said anxiously, "you be sure to catch a gray tomcat and whisk his tail over the bee sting three times."

"That will cure it, will it?" St. John was amused.

"Oh yes, sir, every time. That come down to us from Maggy Figgy herself, and she one of the strongest witches, sir."

St. John pretended to be impressed. "I'll remember it, Mrs. Jones."

Mrs. Jones gave him an apologetic smile. "I know you think it's nonsense, sir, our country ways, but it's the way I was brought up to believe. Superstition, some say, and may be right, but it's hard to lay aside your old beliefs."

St. John looked contrite. "Of course it is, Mrs. Jones. I didn't intend to sound skeptical."

"We shall be wanting dinner at about seven, Mrs. Jones, if you feel like coming over. Please don't feel you must if you're tired," Aunt Daphne said.

"Of course I'll come, madam. Colonel Featherstone brought us the lovely halibut. It should be baked today."

St. John looked interested. "Is the Colonel a fisherman?"

"Oh, only for sport, sir." Mrs. Jones wrapped a wool shawl around her shoulders. "I hope the weather will be good to you. Good day, madam, good day, sir, Miss Daphne." Bowing to them all, she let herself out the back door.

"There!" Aunt Daphne said. "Off to our picnic, children."

20

Daphne had heard about Davidstow, the big air field where American B-52 Flying Fortresses had been based during World War II. It was while he was stationed at Davidstow that her father had met the English Red Cross worker whom he had later married. She was living in nearby Bodmin, sharing a room with her sister Daphne, whose RAF flier husband had been killed in an air battle over the channel less than a year after their marriage.

But Daphne was not prepared for the actual air field. They came upon it unexpectedly from a side road.

"It's enormous!" Daphne said. And as soon as Aunt Daphne pulled the Mini off the road, Daphne got out. On both sides and far in front of them stretched the vast deserted air field, the concrete of its runways now broken and scarred by weeds but seeming still to stretch almost to the horizon.

"They were very large planes, your Flying Forts," Aunt Daphne said. She had gotten out of the car and stood beside Daphne. "They had a great deal of trouble with mist here. The field was abandoned after D-Day." She shaded her eyes, although the sun was not out, and stared far across the empty field as if she were staring into the past.

Daphne had not expected to have any particular reaction to the aerodrome, but she found herself strangely moved. She saw her father in her mind, looking like the picture on her mother's bureau, young and jaunty, in his uniform, with his officer's cap flattened down in the Air Force style, looking as if no war could harm him. And indeed it hadn't.

"Dad was lucky he never got hurt."

Aunt Daphne shook her head. She looked sad and far away. "None of them were lucky. There are many ways of being hurt that don't show." Then she changed her tone abruptly, as if she felt she were being gloomy. "That was the operations hut, over there where you see the foundation. The other buildings are gone now or partly destroyed. The sheep have it to themselves."

All across the wide field sheep grazed, many of them with new lambs, and near Daphne and her aunt a black-bearded goat peered at them inquisitively. Aunt Daphne pointed to a bird, about the size of a jay, that hovered above them on fast-beating wings.

"Kingfisher," she said.

As the bird took off, Daphne saw the flash of red across its chest. She had seen them at home.

After they left the Davidstow moor, Aunt Daphne followed a maze of narrow dirt roads up and down steep little hills until she came at last to a small, beautiful church called St. Clether's. Except for a house across the road, it seemed wholly isolated. Out beyond the graveyard, meadows tilted steeply on the far side of a stile. More sheep grazed here, and the meadow was cut up by their sharp hooves. Down below a stony embankment and across a pretty stream lined with willows, some Jersey cattle lifted their dreamy heads to gaze at the intruders.

St. John, who loved the little Norman churches almost as much as Aunt Daphne did, was enthusiastic. He got his camera and took pictures of the graceful tower and the side of the church.

Before lunch Aunt Daphne took them across one of the meadows to see the Holy Well. It was a spring, with a small stone house.

"Oh, good!" St. John said, dipping his finger in the water and making a cross on Daphne's forehead. "We can drive out the witches."

"Don't be sacrilegious, darling," Aunt Daphne said.

"I'm not. I was serious. I think Mrs. Jones impressed me in spite of myself."

They found a comfortable place to sit on the hillside, and while Aunt Daphne unpacked the lunch, she told them about the many Cornish saints who had come to Cornwall from Wales and Ireland.

"My favorite is the one who was hurled into the sea by the Irish, tied to a millstone. He floated on the millstone to Cornwall."

St. John laughed. "Now that took a bit of doing."

Aunt Daphne offered him a pasty and smiled. "It

could have been done. A lot of that Irish stone is pumice, and pumice floats."

"Daphne, you're outrageous." St. John took a cautious bite of the pasty and looked surprised. "I say! This is very good!"

"Of course it's good. It's delicious. Better hot, of course."

Looking out across the hills, Daphne thought this was one of the prettiest and most peaceful scenes she had ever looked at. She wished she could stay here all afternoon instead of having to go looking for that darned picture, which of course would not be there. No doubt there would be another rude shock of some kind. It was a strange world that held both the quiet beauty of St. Clether's and the sinister threats of witches and thieves. She took a large bite of Mrs. Jones's jam tart and lay back on the grass. The sky was a soft gray and a light breeze pushed the clouds into piled-up masses. Birds that she couldn't identify sang somewhere nearby. Although it was cool, there was a feeling of spring, and the willows along the river had sprouted yellow buds. Aunt Daphne pointed out a plant that looked to Daphne like grass, but which she said was Deptford pink.

"It has lovely red flowers in the summer, something like a small type of sweet william."

Daphne hoped she could see this place later when the wild flowers were sprinkled across the meadows and hills.

21

Aunt Daphne took a slight detour through St. Cleer to show them King Doniert's Stone, a memorial to a king drowned in the nearby Fowey River in 878. In Latin an inscription said: "Doniert has asked prayers for his soul." In country like this, Daphne thought, it would be prudent to ask for prayers for one's soul. St. Cleer was a moorland village, with the bleak rugged landscape of Craddock Moor engulfing it.

The sky had darkened, and the wind had risen, gusting over the moor in chilling bursts. The soft feeling of spring had gone. Daphne remembered Shakespeare's phrase in *Macbeth*—"the blasted heath" where the weird sisters met.

Out of the village they drove up a narrow road and through a series of small valleys and hills to a place where Aunt Daphne turned off.

"We'll have to walk in," she said. "It's all nonsense of course. The painting won't be there." She took her car keys, her small leather purse, and her walking stick. Then after a sharp look around, she locked up

the car. It surprised Daphne for a second that anyone would bother to lock a car out here in this
isolation, but then she remembered why they were
there. You never knew what mischief might be done.

She followed Aunt Daphne up a narrow path,
St. John behind her. No one spoke. Aside from the
tension that kept them still, it would have been hard
to talk in that wind, which was now blowing hard
and steady. April seemed far away out here on the
cold, barren moor.

They walked down several small hills and up
again. The path ended but they kept going across
the grass. They passed a battered wooden sign that
said STONE FARM, but Daphne could see no sign of
any farm. Maybe it had blown away.

Then they passed a band of horses, who watched
them until they were out of sight. The horses graz-
ing out there on that wide, open land made Daphne
think of Arrow, and she felt a stab of homesickness.
Bo had promised to write her about Arrow, after
he went home for Easter.

"There it is," Aunt Daphne said, pointing ahead.

Daphne lifted her head and gasped. The Trethevy
Quoit was much bigger, much more impressive than
she had expected. It was a megalithic tomb built of
tremendous unhewn granite stones. "How did they
ever build that?" she said. All the stones stood upright except for a capstone, which served as a kind
of roof, but which was angled so sharply, it was hard
to believe it could balance there at all in these moor-

land winds, let alone balance there since 1500 B.C. For a moment Daphne wondered if it might be a fake. But that was ridiculous. Who could or would struggle with such a monument?

Aunt Daphne was pointing out to St. John the outline of the burial mound. "This one has two chambers," she said. She led the way inside and showed them where one of the upright stones had been cut at the corner to make a passageway between the two chambers. "Possibly for the spirit of the dead to escape," she said, "or perhaps to leave food for the dead. No one really knows."

St. John was only half listening. He was moving quickly around the monument, looking for the painting. He and Aunt Daphne went outside and poked around the foundation, searching through the grass and weeds.

"Of course there's nothing," he said bitterly. "We knew there wouldn't be."

Daphne was still inside, half-fascinated, half-repelled by this cold, strange tomb, which must have taken such time and strength and patience to build. She backed away and looked up, gasped and then said, "St. John! Aunt Daphne!" When they ducked into the chamber, she pointed up to the jutting corner of one of the upright stones. Just barely visible was the corner of an ornate gold picture frame.

"Daphne! You've found it!" St. John ran his hands up the base of the rock, looking for some kind of handhold. But the stone was perfectly smooth. He jumped up, trying to grab at it, but he couldn't get anywhere near it.

"Give me a boost," Daphne said. "I think I can get it."

"Oh, thank God for tall Americans." He held out his cupped hands for her to put her foot into.

She put her foot into his small hands with some misgiving. "I'll be as quick as I can. I'm kind of heavy."

"Can you lunge upward, dear," Aunt Daphne said. "I'll brace you from the side."

Daphne giggled. She was so nervous and so cold and in a way so scared to be poking around in somebody's tomb like this, but most of all she was proud of herself for having found the picture. She had quite forgotten how sure she'd been that it wouldn't be here.

"Here I go," she said, and heaved herself upward. She felt St. John's hands shake badly and almost give way, but she thrust her long arm up the cold stone in the direction of the picture. Her fingers barely brushed the edge of the frame, but she couldn't grab it, and at almost the same moment St. John's hands wobbled wildly and Daphne had to jump for the safety of the ground.

"Take my stick," Aunt Daphne said, "and sort of poke it over the edge."

"But be careful," St. John said anxiously. "Don't poke a hole in it." He held out his cupped hands again.

"I'll be as quick as I can." Daphne took Aunt Daphne's stick, put her other hand on her aunt's shoulder, and put her foot up and lunged. The stick caught the edge of the picture and swung it toward her. "Here it comes!" She jumped down as the frame came falling.

St. John caught it. His face fell.

"Oh, no!" Daphne said.

"Oh, my dear," Aunt Daphne said to St. John, as if she couldn't stand his disappointment.

The picture frame was empty.

22

They stood in the blowing wind just outside the Quoit. They had searched every accessible inch of the monument. There was nothing more to be found except a note tacked to the frame.

The note was more elaborate than the others. At the top of the page were a snake and a triangle, drawn with a felt pen. Inside the triangle were Aunt Daphne's initials. The letter, typed as usual in lower case, said: "unless you leave, your evil will be returned to you before another month is through." At the bottom of the page was a crescent and a pentangle. As before, there was no signature.

St. John stared off across the unfriendly moor. His hair was tossed in his eyes by the wind. Impatiently he pushed it back, looking utterly miserable. "Well, that's that," he said. "Shall we go?" He started fast up the path toward the car.

St. John drove home, going fast and sometimes it seemed to Daphne rather recklessly. There was little conversation. Daphne sat in the back, and she could see the grim thrust of St. John's jaw in the rear view mirror. She felt somehow guilty, because she had noticed the frame and had got his hopes up. But of course, she reminded herself, it was absurd. It wasn't her fault that the frame was empty.

She was relieved when they got home. As soon as they got out of the car, Constable Carter materialized from the dusk, strolling over to them as if he had just been passing by.

" 'Evening." He touched the hard brim of his tall hat. "A pleasant picnic?"

"Pleasant," Aunt Daphne said, "but unfortunately unproductive, except for these." She took the frame and the note from the car and showed them to him.

"Hmm." he read the note carefully. "The frame is from the painting?"

"Yes. It was on top of one of the standing stones at Trethevy Quoit. My niece noticed it and got it down for us."

"I see." He frowned at the note. "You don't mind if I keep this, madam?"

"No, indeed." She shuddered. "I am glad to be rid of it.

"This is the first time," St. John said, "that the theft of the painting and the witchcraft thing have been plainly connected."

"Quite." Constable Carter smiled ruefully. "And I was the one who was sure there was no connection."

"Nothing to report on this end, I suppose?" Aunt Daphne said.

"Nothing, madam. And Randall seems to have quite disappeared."

Aunt Daphne sighed. "Oh, dear. I shall have to find someone else to see to the dustbins."

"I can do it," Daphne said, but Aunt Daphne looked shocked.

Later she looked startled again when she came upon Daphne in the kitchen after dinner, with her arm around Mrs. Jones's broad shoulders. Mrs. Jones had been weeping into the dishwater because she thought St. John's shortness with her meant that he believed she had conspired with Mr. Randall to steal the painting.

"But that's nonsense," Daphne had said. "No one could possibly think that."

"But the painting is gone," Mrs. Jones said, sniffing and searching in her pocket for a handkerchief, "and Roger Randall is gone, and I'm the one who gave him his alibi. It was me said he left the house when I did and locked up."

"But it's true, isn't it?"

"Yes indeed, every word, as God is my witness." She burst into fresh tears.

It was then that Daphne gave her a hug just as Aunt Daphne appeared in the doorway.

"Mrs. Jones thinks people suspect her," Daphne explained.

"Rubbish," said Aunt Daphne. "No one ever thought such a thing." She sounded cross. "You run along home now, Mrs. Jones. Miss Daphne and I can finish up here."

"But madam . . ."

"Come along now. We'll see you in the morning."

When Mrs. Jones had wrapped herself in her shawl and said tearfully, "Good night, madam, I'm sure," and let herself out the door, Daphne said, "I'm sorry, Aunt Daphne."

"Sorry for what, my dear?"

"Well, I know you people think it's . . . I don't know . . . bad taste or something to get too familiar with . . ." She was unable to use the word "servants." "With the hired help. But to me I don't see the difference. I mean they're people, after all, and working in a kitchen is just as decent and respectable as working in a—a newspaper office or a stockbroker's office, the way I see it. I feel awfully sorry for Mrs. Jones. I can't help it."

Aunt Daphne was looking at her in astonishment. "But surely you don't think I disapprove of your sympathy?"

A little taken aback, Daphne said, "Well, yes, I did. You seem upset."

Aunt Daphne sat down and sighed. "I am upset. St. John is such a love, but when he does get into a temperamental fit, he is so unreasonable. I know he's worried about the money, but money is only money, after all. It's not one's life or one's honor or character or even one's future except in a very strict sense."

"I suppose if you grew up having to worry about money, it seems pretty important."

Aunt Daphne looked at her. "Yes. Quite." She went over to the cupboard. "I came to get some brandy for St. John. I do hope he's not feeling too reckless. Courvoisier is so very dear." She took the bottle of Cognac down from the shelf and got a glass. "And my dear, I was not disapproving of your sympathy for Mrs. Jones. It would be quite beyond my capacities to react as you did, but I am English and you are American."

"I'm glad you're not mad."

"Why should I be? Oh, by the way, the Randall boy is lurking about outside. I presume he may want to talk to you."

"Maybe he has news about his father." Daphne got her jacket, which she had learned to call an anorak, and went out to find Nigel.

23

At first Daphne didn't see Nigel, but in a moment he appeared in front of her.

" 'Allo, where you been?"

"In my house, where else?"

"Nah, you been gone all day."

"Oh. We went on a picnic." She looked at him closely. If his father or his grandmother had had a hand in writing that note and leaving the picture frame, Nigel seemed not to know about it. "Why did you want me?"

"Worried about me dad."

"Oh." She was surprised. He was not given to confiding in her. "Haven't you seen him?"

He shook his head. " 'Fraid they'll kill 'im."

She was startled. "Who would kill him, Nigel?"

"Them."

"Who's them?"

He hesitated a long time. He got a stick and began poking at the dirt around the herbaceous border. Finally he said, "Them Irish."

Daphne tried not to show how interested she was. "Irish?"

"Yah. They give 'im the money."

"What money?"

"For helpin' 'em. Workin' for 'em."

"What did he do for them?"

Nigel looked at her. "I don't know. He never told."

She sat down on the bumper of St. John's car, trying to act casual. Nigel was like a pony that was easily scared off. "Are they the IRA?"

"Nah. The others."

She tried to think what "the others" were called. Ulster Defense? She had been reading about the Belfast troubles in the *Times*, trying to figure it all out. Catholics and Protestants killing each other in particularly gruesome ways. It didn't make any sense to her. And what could Mr. Randall have been doing for the Ulster Protestants, if that was who "they" were? She thought of the Irishman who had come to the cottage looking for Mr. Randall. Was he one of "them?"

"Are there a lot of them?"

Nigel shrugged. "Two or three."

"Nigel, do you have any idea where your father might be?"

"No."

"Did he take my aunt's painting?"

"Don't know. They might make 'im do it for the money."

A car turned into the narrow street, and just before the lights would have picked up Nigel, he disappeared. The car drove slowly by but Daphne couldn't see who was in it. When she looked for

Nigel again, he was gone. She called him but there was no answer.

She went inside. Aunt Daphne and St. John sat in front of the electric fire, St. John looking a little more cheerful. He had a full brandy glass on the floor beside him, and Daphne noticed that the level of Aunt Daphne's precious Courvoisier had dropped considerably. He was doodling on a piece of paper, drawing snakes and crescents and other witch symbols. He looked up and grinned.

"I'm practicing to be a warlock. Isn't there a saying in your country: 'if you can't lick 'em, join 'em?' "

"St. John is feeling a little better," Aunt Daphne said, with a significant glance at Daphne.

"That's good." Daphne decided it wasn't the time to tell them what Nigel had said.

St. John sketched a gruesome head of a witch, mouth open showing one long tooth, hair streaming in the wind, broomstick behind the head. "Old lady Randall," he said, showing it to them. He held it out to the red coil of the heater.

"St. John . . ." Aunt Daphne said.

"It's all right. I won't burn the house down. I just want to incinerate Mrs. Randall."

Daphne watched with a faint sense of horror as the paper caught fire. St. John held it until it burned almost to his hand. Then he dropped it on the hearth.

After a little while Daphne went outdoors again, more because she felt restless than that she expected to see Nigel still there.

She couldn't see him anywhere. Poor little kid. She wished she could help him about his father. Tomorrow she would tell Aunt Daphne and St. John what Nigel had said, but not tonight; they were too upset. She crossed the street and sat on the slate wall that bordered the Paynters' cottage. Absently she put out her hand and jumped. Her hand had leaned on some nettles.

In the misty half-light she peered at her palm, pulling at a nettle. "Ouch," she said aloud.

"Nasty things, nettles."

She jumped. "Oh. It's you, Colonel Featherstone. You startled me."

"I am forever startling you, I fear. I am so sorry. I have been wandering the streets tonight like a ghost." He leaned with both hands on the handle of his walking stick.

"Is anything wrong?" Daphne thought he looked desolate.

"My old dog, my good friend, is dead."

Daphne was genuinely distressed. She knew what it was like to lose a beloved pet, and she could hardly imagine the colonel without his dog. "I am terribly sorry. I know what it feels like."

He gave her a gentle smile. "I thought you would. Well, he was very old for a dog, you see. I was not unprepared."

"But that doesn't help much, does it."

"The death of a friend is never easy. He was all I had left."

"You must get another one, right away. It's the only thing to do."

"Oh, I don't believe I shall, you know. I am getting old myself."

It was the first time he had really looked old. Daphne wished she could help him. "I have a horse that I love very much, and I worry that something might happen to him while I'm gone."

"Try not to worry," he said. "What will be will be. Worry debilitates." After a moment he said, "Did you ever find the tunnel?"

Surprised at the change of subject, Daphne said, "Only a little one that doesn't go anywhere." She told him about the noises in the cellar and the discovery of the short tunnel.

"As for the noises," he said, "I suspect that if you look thoroughly, you'll find kittens in your cellar."

"Kittens?"

"Yes. The Paynters' cat has been searching for a suitable location for her accouchement. I have seen her several times coming and going in the direction of your aunt's cellar."

"Oh, I shall have to look. Aunt Daphne thought it was the cat all the time, but I guess I expected something more melodramatic."

He lifted his head and looked at the half-visible roof of the potting shed. "Have you considered the roof?"

"Pardon?"

"I was just considering, the shed is built up

against the slant of the earth in such a way . . ." He paused, studying it with narrowed eyes. ". . . possibly an outlet into a tunnel, if there were such, would be actually quite high up, to compensate for that slant. Right up under the eaves, for example."

"We never thought of that!" Daphne was excited. "We poked around the floor and the walls . . . Oh, I wonder! . . ."

"It might be worth a look some day." He tipped his hat and was gone up the street before she could remember to say good night. Up near the roof. It could be. On an impulse she decided to go and look.

She opened the garden gate and as she did so, found that Nigel was right behind her. "Nigel! You scared me to death. Were you there all the time?"

He giggled. "Ain't tellin'." He followed her across the garden.

"Don't step on Aunt Daphne's crocuses. Be careful, Nigel. Did you hear what the colonel said?"

"Could be I did, could be I didn't."

"Oh, stop being mysterious." She opened the low door of the shed and felt for the flashlight that Aunt Daphne left hanging from a nail. She switched it on as Nigel came in behind her and closed the door.

While she held the light, Nigel pulled a ladder along the wall, climbing it and poking with his hands along the cobwebbed wall planks just under the eaves. "Toss up a hammer or somethin'," he said. He was all seriousness now. He caught the trowel, which was all she could find that would do, and he

163

carefully knocked at the boards, his head cocked on one side to listen for any difference in sound.

Daphne wondered if Aunt Daphne or St. John could hear them. She doubted it. The dirt bank outside muffled sound. Just wait, she thought, till St. John finds out it was a pregnant cat we were pursuing the other night.

There was only the one wall that abutted the hillside, and Nigel was almost at the end of it. Another frustration. But she saw him tense and then strike the same board again. Even from where she stood, she could hear the difference in the noise the blow made, a sharpness instead of the muffled sound that the other whacks had produced.

"Nigel! Is that it?"

He looked down at her, and his face was half excited, half frightened. "Don't know. Might be just an old rabbit hole." He tugged at the board but he couldn't get hold of a loose end.

"Hit it just off center," Daphne said. "Maybe it will swing open."

He hit it hard with the back of the trowel, just left of center. It gave a little. He pushed, using the heels of his hands, and the board flew inward. "Give us the light," he said urgently. When she handed it up to him, his arm and then his head disappeared into the space left by the board.

Daphne thought she would faint with suspense. Then he backed out, stepping down one step on the ladder, and began to pull hard at the board below

164

the first one. It came loose in a shower of dirt that struck Daphne's upturned face. She brushed it off impatiently. "Is that it? *Tell* me, Nigel!"

He didn't answer. Clutching the flashlight and the trowel he went up the ladder and into the hole. There was a scrabbling sound as he disappeared bit by bit until only the soles of his shoes were visible.

She climbed the ladder. "Nigel, wait for me." But he didn't pause and there was nothing to do but follow him. It took a bit of maneuvering to get her tall frame through the narrow opening. The tunnel was just big enough for her to inch along on her stomach. Nigel's boots were just ahead of her face and she could see the small disk of light from the flashlight. It was a tunnel, all right, and they were in it. As she wriggled along in silence it occurred to her that if it should come to a sudden end, there would be no way to turn around. She swallowed dust and kept her head low.

24

Daphne tried not to think beyond the next few inches. If she went past that, she might panic. Her hands were cut and scraped, the knees of her jeans were torn and her knees scratched, dust filled her throat and made her cough. And worst of all, she thought she was going to suffocate. What a way to go! She was furious with herself for blindly following Nigel into the tunnel without knowing what it was or where it would lead. It was the kind of reckless, unthinking thing she had done at . . . well, at Nigel's age. She thought she had outgrown that sort of thing. No wonder St. John thought she was a child.

She heard Nigel coughing, and then suddenly he came to a stop. She wished he would keep going. If she stopped for long, she didn't think she'd be able to go on again. Nigel at least had the light; she couldn't see anything except the soles of Nigel's shoes. Claustrophobia wrapped its wings around her head and she felt like screaming.

Then something changed. Nigel's soles disappeared and instead she was staring groggily at his ankles, the backs of his legs. For a moment she couldn't understand what had happened. Then she realized. He was standing up.

She pushed at his legs so she could move forward. The change from the cramped tunnel to a cave room big enough to stand up in was so unexpected, she could hardly believe it. She got stiffly to her knees and then bracing herself against the side of the cave, she stood up cautiously, feeling with her hand for the roof so she wouldn't crack her head. It was about an inch above her when she straightened up. She felt giddy.

Nigel was flashing the light around the little room they had come to. It was about five feet long and three and a half feet wide. The roof sloped gradually up.

"Is this the end?" she said.

"Shh." He went to the other end and peered into the darkness. "No. It keeps on goin' and it's higher."

"Thank God," she said. "I couldn't take much more of that." She reached for the light. "Let's have a look."

"No," he said. "Don't shine the torch."

"Why not?"

He shook his head. "Not sure. I think I heard somethin'!"

"You mean, like people?"

"Maybe. I can't tell." He was whispering.

"Maybe it's your dad."

He shrugged, frowning. "Don't know."

"I'll go first now," she said.

"No."

"Yes, Nigel." She took the flashlight from him. If they were going to come upon villains, she'd just as soon know about it first, so she could decide what to do. She moved in ahead of Nigel.

It was much easier now. Although the tunnel narrowed again, and was low enough so she had to stoop, she could walk. She kept the light off, so it wouldn't telegraph their arrival. It was so dark at first that she had to move very carefully, sometimes tripping over loose stones or bumping into the wall of the tunnel.

Then it began to grow almost imperceptibly lighter. She stopped, because now she too heard what seemed to be a murmur of voices. She reached behind her to alert Nigel with a squeeze of the arm. She could feel the tension in him and wished she knew what to expect up ahead. It would be good to have a gun.

She moved forward again, hardly breathing, feeling out each step, before she put her foot down, to avoid sending loose rocks rolling noisily. The tunnel widened again and angled slightly west.

Then there was an abrupt widening and ahead of her in the dim light she could see a small room in the rock. At first she couldn't make out anything. She had stopped so abruptly that Nigel bumped into her. She caught his wrist again and they stood half-crouching.

As her eyes got used to the light, she saw a man

standing back to her with a rifle in his hand. It looked like a 30-30 carbine but she wasn't sure. He held it casually, but it was aimed in the general direction of another man who was sitting on the floor of the cave. That man, she saw, was Mr. Randall, and his wrists and ankles were bound. She heard Nigel's quick intake of breath and she gave him a warning pat.

For several minutes they stood there, keeping very still and trying to hear what was being said. The man with the gun was talking. It seemed odd to see Mr. Randall in that helpless position. It was out of character.

Mr. Randall spoke only once. "I can still drive her out if you give me time," he said.

The man's voice rose. "We gave you time. Now you've got the garda after us because of that damned painting."

The word "garda" puzzled Daphne for a moment until she remembered reading it in the papers. It was the word the Irish used for their police.

The little room was almost full of stacks of boxes like the ones she had seen unloaded from the boat. Guns, of course. Now it seemed so obvious. Mr. Randall had been helping the Irish hide smuggled guns. Either the IRA or the Protestant bunch. Mr. Randall had been trying to get the cottage for them so they could use it to store arms. Probably Mr. Randall had figured he could make use of the painting to get Aunt Daphne to move out.

Nigel touched her arm and pointed to the wall near the far end of the cave. St. John's painting, minus its frame, leaned against the wall. The man with the gun said something sharp to Mr. Randall and then kicked him.

Before she could react to stop him, Nigel threw a large stone, which he had apparently been clutching. It was a perfect shot. It hit the man just behind the ear. He staggered forward and dropped the rifle. Nigel flew through the air as if he had been jet-propelled. He grabbed the gun just as the man regained his balance. The man, and Daphne saw that it was the one who had come looking for Mr. Randall, took one look at Nigel and ran. As he went out through the opening of the cave room, he grabbed the painting and took it with him.

"Son!" Mr. Randall shouted. "Nigel!" He struggled to get up, but he couldn't.

Looking wild and uncertain Nigel hesitated, then put down the gun and ran to his father and felt for the knife that Mr. Randall always wore hanging from his belt. He began to saw at the cords that bound his father.

Daphne grabbed the gun and ran after the Irishman. The tunnel on the far side of the room was much higher and wider and easier to move in. Daphne had the feeling she was nearing the sea. Although she couldn't actually hear the surf, she had some sense of the vibration of it. With the gun in her hand, her head slightly bent to avoid any sudden dips in the tunnel, she loped along as fast as she dared to. For one crazy hysterical moment she saw herself as a character in James Fenimore Cooper, whom she'd always thought was a little ridiculous.

Then she did hear the beat of the sea, and almost at the same moment the quick flapping sound of Nigel's running feet behind her.

She stopped abruptly at the end of the tunnel. The rock opened out in the face of the cliff, about a dozen feet above a small semicircular beach. Above her the cliff rose another fifteen or twenty feet to the surface of the headland. A rope ladder dangled from the cave to within a couple of feet of the sand. Peering down through the misty dark, she saw the Irishman below her. He still held the painting.

"Drop it," she called down to him. When he hesitated, she lifted the rifle. He dropped the painting on the sand and ran toward the thin creamy line of surf that edged the beach.

As he started to angle toward one of the cliffs, Nigel shot past Daphne and jumped to the beach.

"Nigel, come back!" She remembered Aunt Daphne's warning about the speed with which the tide could engulf these little beaches.

But Nigel had cornered the Irishman. He dove at him, catching him around the knees. When the Irishman fell to the wet sand, Nigel began to kick him ferociously.

Keeping a nervous watch on the tide, Daphne shouted again for Nigel to come back. The Irishman shook the boy off and hit him hard. Nigel fell backward onto the beach and lay still. The Irishman suddenly disappeared.

Daphne grabbed the rope ladder and swung down to the beach. The tide sounded suddenly very loud and threatening. It was already coming in well past the entrance to the cove.

Nigel got groggily to his knees just as Daphne reached him. She hauled him up.

"Hurry, Nigel. The tide's coming in."

He glanced quickly at the water. "Run," he said. He grabbed her hand and they ran for the rope ladder. Daphne scooped up the painting as she passed it. Nigel tried to make her go up the ladder first but she shoved him up ahead of her. The spray from the incoming waves was already drenching them.

Nigel scrambled up the ladder and turned to give her a hand. She lifted the painting up to him. As she neared the top of the rope, surf smashed around her legs and tugged at her so hard she was afraid she'd lose her grip. But Nigel had her by the wrists, and in the moment when the surf receded, she dragged herself up and into the mouth of the cave.

She was panting hard. "Will it flood the cave?"

"No. Not this 'un." As if he had suddenly remembered something, he said, "Where'd 'ee go?"

"I don't know. He ran toward that rock and all of a sudden he disappeared."

Nigel looked at the face of the cliff where she pointed. He gave a shivery little grin. " 'E went in the cave."

"What cave?"

"Big cave in there. Floods when the tide's in."

Daphne was startled. "We ought to get him out . . ."

Nigel pointed as a huge wave smashed into the cove, some of it pouring into the opening in the rock where the Irishman had disappeared. She felt shaken. She wiped her salt-wet forehead with her sleeve.

"Do we have to go clear back through the tunnel to get out of here?"

As she finished asking the question, there was a shout from above them and then a bright light shone down.

"Daphne?" It was St. John's voice. "Are you there?"

"St. John!" She had never in her life been happier to hear a familiar voice. "We're here." She picked up her own light and shone it up. She turned to speak to Nigel, but he was gone. "Nigel . . ." She flashed the light back into the cave, but he had already scurried out of sight.

"We're putting down a rope." It was Constable Carter's voice. "Just hang on to it, Miss, and we'll get you up in a second."

It was a heavy double rope knotted in a big loop that she could get her arms through. Holding the painting as carefully as she could, she draped herself over the rope and called up that she was ready.

They brought her up slowly so she wouldn't scrape and bump too badly against the rock face.

173

Once she looked down and saw the black and foaming water that now filled the cove. She thought of the Irishman and quickly looked up again. She hoped Nigel was wrong and that there was some outlet from the cave the man had run into. That was not a way you'd want anyone to die.

St. John and Aunt Daphne, half a dozen policemen, and Colonel Featherstone were waiting for her. Aunt Daphne embraced her, and St. John gave her a big hug. He was almost in tears of relief over the painting.

"I'm geting you all wet and dirty," Daphne said to her aunt.

"Oh, my dear, what does that matter? You're all right! I was so frightened."

"Could someone check on Nigel?" Daphne said to Constable Carter. "He went back into the tunnel. His father . . ."

"We picked up his father in the potting shed," Constable Carter said. "About the UDL man . . ."

Daphne told him what had happened to the Irishman, and the constable said they would check as soon as the tide went out.

"Now you must come home, dear," Aunt Daphne said. "You've been through so much."

As she turned to go, Daphne looked at Colonel Featherstone, who stood a little apart from the others, smiling. "I found the tunnel," she said.

He nodded. "I thought you would." He raised his hat. "Cheerio." And he disappeared into the night.

25

Dear Bo:

It was wonderful talking to you and Mother and Dad on the phone. It must have cost a fortune, I had so much to tell! Aunt Daphne was glad to be able to tell Mother that I am alive and well and, as she likes to say, settling down in Boscastle like an old native. It *is* funny the difference in attitude of the villagers toward us now. They were always very polite and all that, but now they are downright friendly. The women in the paper store where I get Aunt Daphne's *Times* are so chatty and full of local gossip, instead of just saying "Thank you, thank you very much indeed," which is about all they used to say. The greengrocer saves me his best artichokes, and the funny man in the "supermarket" (which is about as big as the cheese section of the Safeway at home) worries about whether the groceries are too heavy for me to carry. Even Mrs. Jones's daughter has warmed up; she saves me her comics. (British comics are really different.)

Mrs. Jones is very relieved to hear how the picture

was taken. Mr. Randall confessed he took it out to the potting shed and later carried it down the tunnel. His plan was to use it to pressure Aunt Daphne into selling the cottage. It was a wild idea, but he was getting scared because the Irishmen were threatening him for not having come through on his end of the deal (to deliver the cottage to them). He got into all this out of greed. The UDL paid him very well because they needed places away from Ireland to build up an arms cache, places that wouldn't get raided. It turns out almost everybody in town suspected something was up and was very worried about the possibility of bombings and violence. They couldn't figure out where Aunt Daphne stood in all of this. (Picture Aunt Daphne as an international provocateuress!) Mrs. Jones feels bad about Mr. Randall because she went to school with him and all that, but she frowns darkly and says, "Them that offers candles to the devil . . ." The body of the UDL man was found in the cave. The other one or two UDL guys got away.

Aunt Daphne spoke to "Sir" at school and now the school bus picks up Nigel. He pretends to hate it, but he is famous for his part in what the papers call a "hair-raising adventure" and he likes that.

St. John drove down yesterday to tell us he sold the Turner for about three times what he paid. He turned pale when Aunt Daphne told him old Mrs. Randall died. He was remembering the caricature of her that he burned. Aunt Daphne looked him in the eye and said, "Now, St. John, the woman was eighty-two and she died of a stroke. Perfectly natural at her age and given her excitable temperament." He said, "Of course, but you did give me a turn."

I persuaded Colonel Featherstone to adopt one of the kittens. I took a calico for myself. She's a love. Did I tell you the colonel was formerly with Army intelligence? He says that's why he's curious about things; he can't kick the habit. Aunt Daphne had him to tea.

Tomorrow I'm going pony-trekking with the chemist's daughter. She has her own ponies. I was very relieved to hear from you that Arrow is okay. I bet he was glad to see you.

The haul the cops got from the tunnel was tremendous. Rifles and pistols and submachine guns and grenades and the stuff to make bombs with (gelignite and all that). It is still very hard for me to understand how people can blow up other *innocent* people, children and mothers and anybody that turns up at the wrong time. I keep remembering reading about the explosion in the Tower of London a couple years back, remember? Kids' faces blown away, a little kid's foot found in the debris, stuff like that happening to kids who had just come to the Tower to see the crown jewels and all that historical stuff. Horrible.

They say a lot of money for the IRA comes from America. I'd like to go on a lecture tour and tell people what happens with their money.

Well, write soon, Bo.

Ta, love.
Daff

P.S.: The *Delabole Press* says I acted like a true Brit!
Aunt Daphne said, "Nonsense and rubbish. You are
a true and valiant Yank."

DAPHNE'S WORD LIST:

ENGLISH:	AMERICAN:
smashing	neat-o
toffs	upper class
blokes	guys
pinta	pint bottle of milk (*which comes in no other size*)
cuppa	cup of tea
ice lolly	popsicle
wellies	rubber boots
i'n it?	isn't it?
loo	toilet
bathroom	room where you take a bath
caravan	house trailer
play a dead bat	deadpan
grass	squeal (tell on)
anorak	outer jacket
blazer	jacket as with skirt or pants
rating	sailor
brolly	umbrella
yard	very tall thin glass of ale (*measures a yard*)
saloon	sedan
marrow	squash
swede	turnip
redundancy	worker out of a job
mod cons	modern conveniences (*as inside plumbing*)
trifle	delicious cake
get your knickers in a twist	get upset (*vulgar usage, Aunt D. says*)
bonnet	car engine
boot	car trunk
were you rung?	did you get a phone call?
wizard	(*see "smashing"*)

AUNT DAPHNE'S WORD LIST:

AMERICAN:	ENGLISH:
neat-o	smashing
guys	chaps
gucky	revolting in a muddy or sticky way
bum lamb	an orphan lamb
barrel-racing	a game involving riding around barrels in relay (?)
bourbon and ditch	whiskey and water (*definition supplied by St. John*)
bourbon and branch	same as above, in Texas
boilermaker	whiskey followed (*"chased"?*) by lager (*defined by St. J.*)
hunky-dory	splendid

180